Angel Takes Off

ALSO BY ROGER SILVERWOOD

ANGEL TAKES OFF

ROGER SILVERWOOD

JOFFE BOOKS

Joffe Books, London
www.joffebooks.com

First published in Great Britain in 2025

Cover art by Nick Castle

ISBN: 978-1-80573-311-9

ONE

Detective Constable Edward Scrivens rushed into Detective Inspector Michael Angel's office, waving his mobile in the air excitedly. 'The judge has given him *thirty* years, sir. It's just been on the news.'

Angel looked up from the report he was reading. 'Madigan? Thirty years?'

He sighed. Thirty years was a long time, but it was far from long enough for Madigan. There wasn't a punishment painful enough to equal the suffering he had inflicted on his victims and their loved ones.

Angel wrinkled his nose. 'That's about two years for every man he has had murdered . . . and he'll cost the state more than a million pounds keeping him safely locked up all that time.'

'Looks in good health, sir.'

'It's all that Caribbean sunshine and good living paid for by the murder, extortion and stealing from the good people of South Yorkshire.'

1

'He'll find prison a bit of a comedown from what he has been used to,' Scrivens said. 'And what will happen to that house, his cars and his boat?'

Angel thought a moment then said, 'The house could become a theatre. It's big enough. The other stuff could be sold off to pay for part of his upkeep in prison.'

'Yes, but it won't be. Any funds raised will go in fees to the judge and the barristers.'

Angel's eyebrows shot up as he realised something he hadn't thought of earlier. 'You know, Ted . . . You're going to go down in criminal history as the detective who got Mad Doug Madigan put away.'

Scrivens smiled, straightened his back, tried to make himself two inches taller and went out of the office, eager to spread the news.

Next day, the *Bromersley Chronicle* headline read: YOUNG COP GETS MADIGAN 30 YEARS. The other media were also very kind to Edward Scrivens, likening him to a modern Sherlock Holmes.

At his house, Scrivens came down the stairs at eight the following morning with the *Bromersley Chronicle* under his arm, whistling something indistinguishable to his wife and probably himself.

'Seen the paper?' he said as he walked into the kitchen proudly smiling and unfurling the newsprint on the table.

She couldn't understand why he was so pleased.

'Yes,' Gillian Scrivens said disinterestedly. She was a small, pretty, nervous young woman.

The headline caught her eye. 'Congratulations,' she said because she thought that's what he wanted her to say.

She quickly read the report, observed the photo of him then said, 'Very good. But why didn't you change into your best suit for the photo?'

At 8.20, they bustled out of the house together to his car parked on the short drive at the side of their semi-detached. He dropped her off at Wells Street school gates.

'Be kind to the kids, darling,' he said with a grin.

She smiled.

'And you be kind to all you interview,' she said as she leaned over to give him a kiss.

The kiss lasted longer than either expected. Neither knew the reason why.

A warm feeling spread across his chest. He didn't want to leave her.

Gillian said, 'Goodbye, darling. Got to go.'

Scrivens watched her open the gate, go through it and then close it. He smiled and reflected on how lucky he was, then he engaged a gear and let in the clutch.

He made his way along a back road through countryside which was a short cut to Bromersley Police Station.

On that quiet back road was a long-established cart track that crossed the tarmac. Farmers had used it for years. On the cart track, either side of the road, was a large black car with two big men in each. Both drivers had their phones to their ears and both cars had their engines running.

Scrivens, unaware of what was ahead, meandered along this route well known to him singing, 'O what a beautiful morning, O what a beautiful day.'

He drove the car round a curve and saw a car poking its nose from behind the hedge, then another on the opposite side came into view.

He stopped singing, slowed down and wondered what was happening.

Then the two black cars met gently nose to nose and stopped, completely blocking the road.

He had to stop. He sat there puzzled by the hold-up. He looked round to see if there was anyone on foot who might explain what was going on. There was nobody. His face muscles tightened. He banged on the steering wheel with fists clenched a few times. Then he got out of his car and approached the nearest of the two black cars. He saw the driver's face. He recognised it instantly. His heart dropped down to his stomach and bounced. It was Aaron Penn, one of the heavies from Mad Doug Madigan's gang.

Aaron was a giant of a man, thought to have murdered his first wife by throwing her down a flight of stairs and her mother by putting her head in a gas oven. However, neither offence was ever proved.

Scrivens was breathing deeply and quickly. He felt a jab in his back. It was the muzzle of a gun.

A high-pitched voice said, 'Put your hands up where I can see them.'

It was the squeaky voice of Bennie Jones. He had a voice like a table fork being scraped on a bone-dry plate.

* * *

An hour later, as Detective Inspector Michael Angel was in his office at Bromersley Police Station with Detective Sergeant Flora Carter dealing with the morning's post, a brick smashed through the office window. Glass flew in all directions as the missile hit Angel's desk then landed on the floor.

Angel ran out into the corridor, down to the back door of the station, raced out onto the private police car park, out into the street and along the pavement. He saw a big black car turn round a corner and disappear out of sight. He stopped running. He knew he couldn't have caught it.

4

His face wrinkled with annoyance and disappointment. He stood on the pavement panting. Arms akimbo, he stared along at the terrace houses where he had last seen the rear of the car. Then his lips tightened. He gave a mighty sigh, and still breathing heavily, returned to his office.

DS Carter had the wastepaper basket in her hand, and was looking round the room. She had binned most of the glass from the smashed window but there were still shards turning up.

'Any luck?' she said.

'I saw the car. It was black and big and typical of the sort that Madigan ran about in.'

Angel saw that the missile was half a house brick with an envelope fastened to it with tape.

He reached out to his desk, opened a drawer, and took out a pair of white linen gloves. He put them on, then picked up the brick. With one snip of the scissors he released the message. He carefully opened he envelope and unfolded the single sheet of paper inside. There was a message handwritten in block letters. It said:

RELEASE MR MADIGAN IF YOU WANT TO SEE EDWARD SCRIVENS ALIVE.

Angel's face went white. He felt a small, hot lump of pain in his chest. It was spreading fast and throbbing like a big bass drum. Still holding the paper, he looked across the room seeing nothing.

Carter saw his expression and said, 'What's it say?'

Then she looked over his shoulder and read the paper. Then suddenly she gasped and said, 'Oh no! Madigan's mob have kidnapped Ted Scrivens.'

* * *

At 10 o'clock that same morning, patrolman PC Sean Donohue brought a bald-headed little man through the double doors of Bromersley Police Station, along the corridor to the Charge Room and up to the duty sergeant's desk.

'Careless driving, Sergeant,' the patrolman said.

The little man protested, gesticulating wildly with open hands. 'I keep telling him I've done nothing wrong.'

Sergeant Clifton turned to look at the little man and was taken aback to see that he knew him. 'Is it Moxey again?'

The little man looked at Clifton, jerked back his head in surprise and said, 'I don't know who *you* are, or how you know who I am, because I have never seen you before in my life.'

'You are Arnold Moxey. Accused of dealing cannabis with three others,' Clifton said. 'Four or five years ago. You got off with a warning.'

'I got off because I didn't do it.'

Clifton then turned away to Donohue. 'Have you breathalysed him?'

Moxey said, 'I'm as sober as a judge.'

'He *was under* the limit, Sarge.'

Clifton frowned, looked at Donohue and said, 'Do it again.'

Moxey glared at the sergeant and said, 'I'm missing fares while I'm in here, you know. And business isn't too good anyway.'

Moxey moaned, shook his head and said, 'I haven't had a drink all morning. What does it take to convince you?'

The sergeant then pushed a form into Donohue's hand and said, 'Take him into Interview Room number 2A. The new one.'

Interview Rooms 2A and 2B were next door to Angel's office which Angel found convenient. However, to make another interview room because sometimes they had been short of rooms, Interview Room 2 had recently been divided into 2A and 2B with a wooden wall and a door between them. It was necessary to walk through 2A to reach 2B which was sometimes a disadvantage. Also, sometimes if voices were raised a little, one could hear what was being said in the next room.

'Come on, Moxey,' Sean Donohue said. 'Let's get started on this statement.'

* * *

At 10.20 a.m., DS Flora Carter came quickly into Angel's office with a paper file.

Angel held his hand out for it. He took it and began scanning the pages.

'What are we going to do, sir?' Carter said.

Angel turned away. 'We do our best, Flora.'

Then suddenly, the door opened and Gillian Scrivens rushed in, followed by another female police officer.

Angel jumped up.

Her eyes were wet and red. She wrapped her arms round Angel's neck and sobbed, 'Oh, Michael!'

The other woman was PC Leisha Baverstock, who had been appointed to be with Gillian Scrivens twenty-four/ seven for her protection and to keep Angel informed of any developments.

'I couldn't stop her, sir,' Leisha said.

Gillian continued to weep, so Angel pulled her close to his shoulder.

His chest felt like an open wound. His muscles tensed. He couldn't think of anything comforting to say to her. He was angry with himself for being so useless.

She just held him close so he could smell her hair.

Eventually, she relaxed the embrace and Angel found he could relax too.

They separated.

She wiped away her tears with a tissue.

'What are you going to do, Michael? I know you can't just let Madigan walk, but Ted—' Her voice broke.

Angel bit his bottom lip. 'Oh, Gillian, I wish it was as simple as that.'

The young woman's eyes flashed. 'I need him back.'

'I know, Gillian,' Angel said. 'But it's taken years to capture Madigan and find a charge that we could make stick. The police have to show strength and solidarity to millions of honest, decent, law-abiding citizens.'

'They'll murder Ted, if—'

'Gillian, you must believe that justice will prevail and that the court and the police will find a way to . . . out of this.'

'I just want him back,' Gillian said tearfully. 'Did he tell you he's going to be a dad? I'm expecting in September. I don't want my firstborn to be without . . . without a father.'

Angel's heart strings could not have been pulled much tighter.

'You know I won't let that happen, Gillian,' he said. 'I'll move heaven and earth to bring him home safe to you and the baby. Now go back home with Leisha. I will keep you informed.'

Leisha stepped forward.

'Michael,' Gillian said, 'promise me that Ted is going to be all right.'

'Everybody is doing their best, Gillian,' Leisha said.

'Promise me that you'll get Ted out of their clutches and that he'll come home soon.'

'Time is very short, Gillian. Leave us to get on with the business of working hard to get Ted free. Go back home with Leisha.'

Leisha stepped forward and said, 'Come on, Gillian. Grab hold of my arm. Let Inspector Angel get on with the job.'

'How is Michael going to get my Ted back without releasing Madigan?'

'It's going to be all right, Gillian,' Leisha said. 'We have had similar situations to deal with before. Stop worrying. It will be all right.'

Gillian was not convinced. She cried even louder and longer as Angel waved his hand to Leisha to take Gillian Scrivens away.

The policewoman led the sobbing woman out of Angel's office.

Angel turned away and swallowed. He knew he had to make some tough decisions and he had to make them quickly.

'Flora,' Angel said. 'We are short of time. Do we know who is taking over running Madigan's interests?'

'I don't know,' Flora said.

'There's his personal bodyguard. It'll be one of those who are behind the kidnapping. The note was well written. It is far more professional than our regular thug. Take note, there are no spelling mistakes and the punctuation is correct.'

'There's Aaron Penn, Bennie Jones . . . there's a couple more. I can't remember their names.'

'They're not the brains of the outfit. Put them all together and they couldn't pass the eleven plus.'

Angel reached out for the phone and tapped in a number. A voice soon answered. 'Simon Twelvetrees, Crown Prosecution Service. Can I help you?'

Angel said, 'We've got a problem, Simon. Can you join us? It concerns the situation of our man, Edward Scrivens.'

'Horrible business, Michael. I've just heard. Oh yes. I'll come straight away,' Twelvetrees said.

Twelvetrees was a barrister and frequently assisted Angel in drafting charge sheets and other legal matters. When he arrived, Angel questioned him straight off. 'Simon, you have been looking into Madigan's business affairs. Have you come across anyone there that could be said to be capable of putting a kidnapping plan together?'

Twelvetrees pursed his lips. 'There's his crooked accountant, Jacob Grant. He can make two and two add up to five. He seems very intelligent — he may be, but he is far more involved in the criminal side of his affairs that the title suggests.'

Angel winced. 'Jacob Grant?'

'That's the one, Michael. The rest are only muscle.'

'Which one has the most to lose if Madigan is *not* returned to them?'

'All of them. You are putting me in an impossible position,' Twelvetrees said.

Angel shook his head. 'I know. I know. Let's put it another way. Who do you think expects to succeed Madigan once they realise that he is going to prison and he isn't coming out?'

'Definitely Jacob Grant.'

Angel said, 'Do you still believe that Jacob Grant is heir apparent in that dreadful gang?'

'Could be.'

'And he will know where Ted Scrivens is being held?'

'Of course. I expect he planned the kidnap.'

Angel looked thoughtful.

Twelvetrees said, 'It's only what I *think*, Michael. I may be wrong.'

'Hmm. But I don't think you are,' Angel said. 'Excuse me a minute.'

He turned away and snatched up the phone. 'This is very urgent. John,' he said, 'pick up Jacob Grant for questioning.'

* * *

Meanwhile, from Interview Room 2A . . .

Arnold Moxey wiped his perspiring forehead and gripped the four pages of questions he had to answer. 'I don't know why I have to answer all these questions.'

'Let's tell the truth, shall we?'

'I always tell the truth.'

'It doesn't say that here.'

'Well, er, they've got it wrong.'

'There's a first time for everything, Moxey,' Patrolman Sean Donohue said. 'Come on. Let's finish this.' He looked down at the form. 'It says, "Place of birth."'

Moxey said, 'What's that got to do with driving, I ask you? I was born in Barnsley, bottom of Racecommon Road.'

'It only needs to know the country. I will put UK.'

'I was born in *Barnsley*. That's *England*. *Put England*.'

Donohue's lips closed tight together. 'I've put UK. It's quite correct. Next question?'

TWO

It was 10.40 a.m.

DS Flora Carter, Sergeant 'Bernie' Clifton, Mr Simon Twelvetrees and DS Donald Taylor were with Angel in his office, when the phone rang.

He reached out for it. 'Angel,' he said.

It was PC John Weightman. 'I've got Jacob Grant in reception, sir. Where do you want him?'

Angel had a fluttery sensation in his chest and his heart-beat raced.

'Put him in Interview Room 2B and stay with him, John,' he said. 'I'll see you there in a couple of minutes.'

Angel put the phone down, turned to the four and said, 'Jacob Grant is here.'

They answered almost in unison, 'Good.'

Angel sighed. He wasn't looking forward to meeting Grant. And yet he was. He was anxious to get Ted Scrivens back safely. He turned back to Twelvetrees and said, 'Will you join me?'

Twelvetrees smiled and nodded.

Angel's pulse was racing. He didn't want to make any mistakes.

The two men made their way out of his office to the interview rooms next door.

Angel said, 'I am sorry for disturbing you, Sean, but we urgently need 2B beyond to interview a man. We'll try not to disturb you.'

Donohue smiled and said, 'Thank you, sir. But you must come and go as you need. John Weightman and another have just gone through.'

Moxey suddenly looked at Angel and kept his eyes on him and said, 'Are you that famous inspector who is sometimes on TV and in the papers?'

Angel looked at Donohue for help.

Donohue said, 'Yes, he is. And he's very busy with a big case now . . . and he won't want to hear you rabbiting on through the wall.'

Moxey pushed his advantage. 'You mean he hasn't time to consider injustices being carried out under his very nose, and he wouldn't take any notice of a little man being wrongly accused of careless driving?'

Angel turned to Donohue and said, 'Have you got video of this driving?'

'Yes, sir. Clear as day.'

Then Angel turned to the little man and said, 'Sorry, Moxey. Sounds like a cast-iron verdict of guilty to me.'

Angel and Twelvetrees went into the adjoining Interview Room 2B.

Immediately Angel saw Jacob Grant seated at the table.

Jacob Grant was a slim, middle-aged man in an immaculately tailored dark suit, collar and tie. He had a full head of dark brown, wavy hair, was clean shaven, and he had sharp-cut facial features sometimes associated with Teutonic nations.

The presence of Grant made Angel's stomach and chest flood with anger momentarily. He cleared his throat, looked directly at Grant and then pointed to a chair at the table.

Grant sat down and said, 'I'll have it understood that I am not under arrest. I am here voluntarily . . . to help police with their inquiries.'

'Understood,' Angel said drearily.

He first had them seated at the table. 'Come in, John. Sit here. Mr Grant here. Simon over there.'

Angel went through the introductions and then began.

'Mr Grant, what was your relationship with Mr Madigan?'

'I am his accountant,' Grant said. 'I advise him on tax matters and I supervise some of his businesses. Having said that, if this is a formal interview, I am entitled to have my solicitor present.'

'Indeed you are,' Angel said. 'But I am not intending this interview to be formal. Today this meeting is *not* being recorded. I will be asking questions only about Detective Constable Edward Scrivens. I hope he is in good health.'

'He is being very well looked after. You may have no fear in that respect. We are naturally worried about the health and comfort of our Mr Madigan.'

'He is his usual vital self,' Angel said. 'When do you propose releasing our man, Edward Scrivens?'

'The moment you release Mr Madigan,' Grant said. 'It is as simple as that.'

Angel said, 'That would be very difficult.'

'Difficult?' Grant snapped. 'I thought that this deal could done between you and us quietly and quickly . . . before the public and the press became aware of the facts. I don't know what the delay is.'

'There is no delay,' Angel said. 'Just wanting clarity. That's all. When did you last see Edward?'

Angel reckoned that a straight answer might indicate the length of time to get there and therefore provide a clue to the place where they were holding Scrivens prisoner.

But Grant was ready for such a question. His lips tightened. 'I've already told you, he is in fine form.'

'I wanted to know *when* you last saw him. Was it last night or this morning?'

Grant pursed his lips, blew out an impatient sigh and then said firmly, 'Scrivens is in very good form. Take my word for it.'

But Angel knew he couldn't take any word that Grant had said for granted.

Grant looked at his watch then at Angel and said, 'Look, Inspector, I just think you are wasting time.'

'No, sir,' Angel said. 'I think you are wasting *my* time. We have only had a few minutes to consider your proposal.'

'We also expect our Mr Madigan to be given the best of everything. What else is there to consider? How much longer do you want?'

Angel blinked then said, 'This is the police. Unusual situations like these have to go through official channels. It takes a little time.'

'How much time?'

'A week or two.'

Jacob Grant's voice went up an octave. '*A week or two! A week or two!* Sounds as if we may have to rough Scrivens up a bit.'

Angel clenched his teeth, and then said, 'Don't you touch a hair on that man's head.'

'If I remember, I'll phone you in a day or two.' Grant stood up to leave, suddenly calm and controlled.

Angel said, 'Before you go, I need to impress on you the need to look after Ted Scrivens. Give *him* the best of everything. I can assure you that Mr Madigan is being very well treated.'

Grant rubbed his chin thoughtfully, then said, 'Can I see him?'

'Not possible,' Angel said.

'He's safe and comfortable . . . and it's best he is not disturbed.'

Grant was a wily old bird.

But so was Angel.

Grant pulled a face and sat down. He wanted Madigan.

And Angel wanted Scrivens.

Angel met Grant's hard stare with an equally steely glance.

* * *

Some of the exchanges next door had been heard through the silences . . .

'Now then, Moxey, we've finished the form,' Patrolman Sean Donohue said loudly and firmly. 'You've just to sign it in two places, there and there, and then initial each page at the bottom to validate them.'

Moxey murmured something that sounded like 'breeding incense' and then there was silence.

'Let's have a look at what you've done.'

There was the scraping of the legs of a chair on the floor as Moxey pushed himself away from the table.

There were a few seconds' silence then Donohue angrily said, 'You've signed it in the *wrong* place. You've signed it where the witness has to sign it.'

Moxey said, 'That's right, isn't it? After all, I am the witness.'

16

'No,' Donohue said. 'You're the *subject* of the form. You have advised us of the facts and *I* am the witness.'

The corners of Moxey's mouth turned down.

'How much longer is this going to take?' he said. 'I've my business to run . . . money to earn.'

* * *

Aaron Penn pressed the catch on his Glock handgun and the magazine dropped out of the handle into his hand. He opened the box of bullets and began feeding them into the magazine until it was full. It held sixteen. Then he tucked the gun into his waistband and nodded at what he had achieved.

Bennie Jones was lounging on the other bed in the double-bed hotel room holding *The Sporting Life* to his face, but not reading it.

'Expecting trouble?' he said.

Penn's grim face told Jones that all was not well.

Penn then waved his arm around the room.

'Who's paying for this posh hotel and room service?' he said. 'I hope it's not coming out of my pot.'

'Grant knows what he's doing,' Jones said. 'The police will not be looking at a posh pad like the Feathers Hotel for a family of three, father, son and invalid woman in a wheelchair. They'll be looking for three *men*.'

Penn frowned at this. 'I hope you're right.'

'It's time to look at "mother". See if he's still asleep. He might be needing another jab.'

Jones stood up and shambled across the room to a door into another bedroom.

It was another single bedroom, part of the suite, pleasantly furnished and decorated, but smaller.

He quietly approached a wheelchair in the centre of the room. The slim figure of Edward Scrivens was slumped in an untidy heap in the chair, his eyes closed and his head on one side. His eyes were closed and he was breathing slowly and regularly. The top part of him was wearing a colourful woman's blouse and the lower half his own suit trousers. He was partly covered with a tartan car rug. A big, mousey-coloured woman's wig had slipped and was positioned lopsided on his head. His left wrist was anchored to the arm of the wheelchair by handcuffs. A syringe and several ampoules were on the dressing table on an open holdall.

Jones watched Scrivens a few seconds, then he returned to the bigger room.

Penn looked up at him.

'Sleeping like a baby,' Jones said.

Penn said, 'Why doesn't Grant contact us? What the hell is he playing at? They can't still be talking. All they had to do was agree on a time and a place.'

'I hope he brings the boss back with him, and that they've not just arrested him.'

'I thought that . . . but they wouldn't do that. They have to set an example. Whatever the cops do, they have to come out of this smelling of violets.'

Neither man spoke for a minute or so then Jones, putting his hands in his jacket pocket, came out with a pack of cards in a well-worn cardboard box. He looked across at Penn and said, 'Poker?'

Penn looked up. He pulled a face of discontent. 'Doesn't anything ever bother you? Out there, there's Grant. A uni man. Brains of the nation. Talking over our future. Whatever he agrees to, we'll have to agree to. Yet we have no idea what's happening.'

'I don't like Grant, but I trust him,' Jones said. 'And all your rabbiting don't make the time pass more quickly.'

Penn's lips tightened turning his mouth into a snarl, then he said, 'He could easily save his own skin by doing a deal and selling us down the river.'

'He wouldn't do that,' Jones said thoughtfully. Then his face changed. The corners of his mouth turned downwards. 'Would he?'

After a few moments, Jones reached forward to the top of the bed and pulled a handgun out from under the pillow.

Penn saw what he was doing and so he passed the half-full box of bullets to Jones.

Jones took it, clicked to release the gun's magazine and began to load it.

* * *

Angel stood up, crossed the interview room to Twelvetrees. They had an urgent whispered exchange. Then Angel made for the door.

In the interview room next door, Donohue looked across from the desk and Moxey.

'Sorry to interrupt, Sean,' Angel said.

'Are you making any progress, sir?' Donohue said.

'Oh yes,' Angel said, with a wink and then forcing a smile. '*We've got a deal with Grant. He's singing like a canary.*' Donohue caught Angel's wink as he turned to whisper loud enough for Moxey to hear: 'We get Ted Scrivens back and we keep Madigan, as if that had ever been in doubt. Then Jacob Grant also goes free.'

Angel's plan was that Madigan's gang would think that Jacob Grant had done a deal with the police that betrayed them but let Grant off all charges and let him go a free man.

Moxey's eyes grew noticeably bigger with every word that Angel had said.

Angel looked for the little taxi driver's reaction and was delighted. Angel then went out of the room with a smile on his face.

Moxey and Donohue exchanged glances of surprise.

Angel dropped the smile when he reached the corridor and his office where he summoned DS Flora Carter and Sergeant 'Bernie' Clifton.

Angel said, 'Spread the word. Pretend it is true, to be confidential and look delighted.'

Then he made an internal phone call to Donohue in the interview room.

'You know what to do, now, Sean. Release Moxey and look cheerful,' Angel said into the mouthpiece.

Donohue forced a grin and in a voice that Moxey could clearly hear said, 'That's great news, sir. I am glad that Grant has done a deal. It's a relief knowing that I'll see Ted Scrivens again.'

Donohue watched Moxey's face register all that he was saying.

Then he replaced the receiver and turned to Moxey, smiling. 'Aren't you a lucky man? I've just been instructed to give you a warning, which I have already done and to release you without charge, so hop it and don't let me see you breaking the law again.'

'Yes,' said Moxey promptly.

He couldn't get out of that police station fast enough to dodge round the corner and make a phone call to the Madigan nest to deliver the 'news'.

* * *

Minutes later, Angel went down the station corridor, past the cells, to the rear door. He silently opened it two centimetres and peered out on to the private police car park and pound. It was almost full of cars and quiet. There was the occasional car arriving or one leaving. The yard light caught the two menacing heads bobbing up from time to time behind a car bonnet. It was regretful that there was nothing he could charge them with.

He nodded approvingly. It must have been the first time he was pleased to see two armed crooks 'concealed' so near the station.

He closed the back door and went up the corridor to the other side of the police station, then to the front window and looked through it. He made a slow, panoramic scan of the much busier road with traffic passing most of the time. Beyond that, on the opposite side of the road, several cars were parked. One of the cars had the driver's window open and a familiar face was looking his way. He was holding a mobile phone to his ear. He was huge. It was Aaron Penn!

Angel smiled grimly as his heart thumped away. Penn was no doubt being given the fake news.

Then he noticed two big men on the pavement. They had been walking in opposite directions and had met on the pavement outside the police station. He recognised one of them. It was Bennie Jones. Both men waited for an opportunity, then crossed the road and went up to Aaron Penn in the car.

Angel had seen what he expected and had hoped to see. He turned and went back to Jacob Grant and Simon Twelvetrees in the interview room.

He glanced at Twelvetrees and quizzically raised his eyebrows.

Twelvetrees shook his head with a small quick jerk to indicate there had been no new developments.

Grant looked at Angel then stood up. 'I must leave,' he said. He sniffed. 'We have made no progress whatsoever. You've been all talk but no action.'

Angel reached out to the landline phone and said, 'I'll organise a car to take you.'

'Don't bother,' Grant said, raising his nose in a very superior way. 'I have my own.'

He took out his mobile phone, scrolled up to a telephone number, clicked on it and put it to his ear.

'Is that Aaron?'

'Yeah?'

'Send my car to pick me up straight away,' Grant said.

There was a short pause then down the phone line Aaron Penn said, in mock innocence, 'What sort of a deal have you got, boss?'

Grant glanced at Angel, turned away, and said into the mouthpiece, 'I'll tell you everything when I return.'

Penn couldn't continue the pretence.

'You needn't bother,' Penn said. 'All the gang knows that you've sold us out. The next time I see you . . . you'd better have a gun!'

Then the line went silent.

Grant frowned and closed the phone. He thought a moment or two then turned to Angel and said, 'All the cars seem to be in use at my end. There seems to be a problem. Would you get me a taxi after all?'

Angel was delighted. The plan was working. Although he hadn't heard both sides of the conversation, it was apparent to him that Penn was far from pleased with Grant. The plan was working.

'I'll organise a lift,' he said. 'Excuse me. Won't be a minute.'

22

Angel went out of the office briefly and then returned.

'There'll be one along very soon,' he said.

Angel led Grant in silence out of the interview room, up the corridor, through the security door and past the Inquiry Desk.

As soon as Jacob Grant saw the front door he stepped forward quickly, overtaking Angel and without saying a word, walked out into the daylight and down the stone steps.

Angel wrinkled his nose. He quickly turned round and made for the security door. He flashed his card at the screen and it opened. It was then that he heard pistol shots. Two reports in quick succession.

He stopped. He sighed deeply. He felt that he should be delighted. But he wasn't. He had expected it, but he was sad. Hopefully the two shots had been exchanged exclusively between members of the Madigan gang. Any elimination of anybody from that mob had got to be good.

By the time Angel reached his office, his phone was ringing. He hoped it might be from or about Ted Scrivens. Must not forget that all these arrangements were to engineer the release of him unharmed.

His hand was shaking slightly as he reached out for the handset. 'Angel,' he said boldly into the handset.

It was Detective Superintendent Horace Harker, Angel's immediate superior. Not one of Angel's favourite people.

'I've had a report that there had been some pistol shots heard outside the front of the station,' he said. 'From my window I can see that there is a man prostrate on the pavement who appears to be either wounded or dead. It doesn't make the service seem at all attractive with pistol shots and bodies decorating the front of the station. Deal with it.'

'Yes, sir.'

When Angel arrived on the concrete forecourt, there was a small group of people around the body of Jacob Grant, comprising two elderly women who stood muttering to each other and two PCs from reception.

Grant was motionless, his white striped shirt scarlet with blood. Angel felt for a pulse on his neck . . . there was none.

Angel's lips tightened across his teeth. He had allowed Grant to die before finding out Edward Scrivens' whereabouts.

He summoned DS Carter to deal with the killing. Then made his way back to his office.

Angel was not happy.

The plan had failed.

Then he returned to his office and began the report.

About twenty minutes later Angel's phone rang out.

'I am the Assistant Manager of the Feathers Hotel,' a young man said, 'I have to report a man dressed as a woman. He *says* he is a policeman and his name is Edward Scrivens. He is inextricably fastened to a wheelchair and has been resident in suite number one with two others who have now vacated the suite without paying the bill. They have run up a high bill and Mr Scrivens says that I should report the matter to you. Would you please come down to sort all this out?'

Angel beamed. The plot had not failed. He dashed across town to the Feathers Hotel to recover Ted Scrivens.

It was the beginning of the end of Madigan's gang.

THREE

In another part of Bromersley . . .

A young couple lay on a couch in the dim light, snuggled close with their arms around each other.

'Are you sure we'll be alone, sweetheart?' the young man said.

'Positive. Both Mum and Dad always play Bridge on a Wednesday night. They won't be back until around ten thirty.'

After a few moments, the young man said, 'Did you talk it over with your Mum?'

There was a slight hesitation in her reply.

'I dared not tell Mum everything, but I did say that we wanted to get married as soon as possible. But she said I was too young, and that in any case my dad wouldn't give his consent. And she's right. He's old fashioned. He *won't* give his consent.'

'We don't need his consent, darling. We can go to Gretna Green and find—'

'Oh, darling,' she said. 'Could we?'

She kissed him again and they cuddled up even closer.

His hand ran firmly up her legs, beyond the knee, caressing her thighs.

'Darling,' he said as they broke away. 'We can go up to Gretna Green, get married then go away for a few days . . . then after six months, there'll be the baby. It'll be a *fait accompli*. He can't do anything about it.'

'Oh darling, that'd be magic.'

They kissed again.

'Oh, darling,' she said.

'You didn't tell them you were expecting . . . ?' he said.

'I daren't. I don't know what my dad would say.'

'He's behind the times. He doesn't realise—'

He stopped talking abruptly then said, 'Did you hear that?'

'Hear what?'

'I thought I heard a car door.'

'It could be one of next door's.'

Then there was the distinct sound of the front door being opened and closed.

The young man's jaw dropped open.

He gasped and said, 'It's your father!'

Then the room's door was being opened.

The young man's eyes were wide open and bulging.

The shadow of a hand holding a gun showed on the wall by the open door.

There were two loud gun shots.

The young man's chin dropped down on to his chest.

The girl screamed.

'Cut!' a voice from behind the cameraman called.

Spotlights were doused and the house lights, up in the ceiling of the sound stage, were switched on.

The score or so of actors and crew on set relaxed, some sighed and some began talking among themselves.

After a few words with the camera crew, the German film director, Edward Schultz, said, 'All right, that's OK.' Then he turned to the floor manager and said, 'Dick, have the painters finished the set for the pub scene?'

'Yes. All done, Mr Schultz.'

'Ten minutes and we'll move onto scene three two two.'

Through a loudspeaker, a dominant voice said, 'Take ten. Then camera rehearsal scene three two two.'

The chatter and working noises of the set builders, technicians and electricians was suddenly, unexpectedly interrupted by a loud, chilling scream. It came from Samantha Rock.

'Oh my God!' she cried.

The sound stage went silent.

All eyes turned towards her.

Schultz looked up over his spectacles, blinked and said, 'We've finished recording, Samantha.'

Samantha Rock, face perspiring through the make-up, was standing by the couch where she had been filming. She was looking down at the body of Rodney Pertwee. Blood was seeping from his head onto the couch.

* * *

Detective Inspector Michael Angel and Detective Sergeant Flora Carter arrived at the reception gate in the DI's BMW. They were waiting at the 'In' gate outside a white building of the Northern Film Studios. It was one of eight new buildings comprising the NFS site on the York Road four miles out of Bromersley.

As Angel waited at the barrier, he saw a grey-haired woman in a light raincoat, green velvet hat, square-heeled leather shoes, brown stockings and carrying a brown paper carrier bag. She walked straight through the 'Out' gate.

At the same time, a uniformed man came out of the island between the 'In' and the 'Out' gates and leaned over to the open window of Angel's BMW.

Angel flashed his warrant card and badge and said, 'Police. We're responding to a triple nine call.'

The man said, 'Oh yes, sir. Awful. Sound Stage Two, that's straight on, it's on your left.'

'Thank you,' Angel said and pressed the button to close the car window.

The uniformed man hastily lifted the barrier.

Angel drove to a marked-out parking space outside the sound stage building with the big figure '2' painted on its facing corner.

He locked the car and guided Carter round to the sound stage door. He pulled it open and they found themselves in an anteroom. There were coloured lights above a door and notices on the door saying do not enter when red light is showing.

'The light's green, sir,' Carter said.

Angel nodded and pulled open the door. They went into an enormous building with a collection of caravans, props, scenery, technical equipment and people occupying some of the vast floor space.

Most of the cast and crew were around the body on the couch.

Edward Schultz was talking to a man in shirt sleeves.

Angel approached them. Schultz saw him coming. He broke off the conversation and said, 'Are you from the police?'

'Inspector Angel,' he said. 'This is Sergeant Carter. A Mr Schultz reported a murder?'

'That's me,' Schultz said, then quickly reported what had happened. He took him over to where Rodney Pertwee's body still lay.

Angel looked down at the body. He had seen many over the years, but he never got used to it. He breathed in quickly and resolved to get on with the job.

'What time was this?' Angel said.

'About twenty minutes ago,' Schultz said. He looked at his watch. 'So, about eight forty-five.' He looked up for someone to confirm his estimation.

Several willing voices said, 'That's right,' 'About that,' and 'Eight forty-five on the dot.'

DS Flora Carter noted it down.

'Thank you.' Angel took out his phone, scrolled down to a number. It was soon answered.

'Scrivens,' Angel said. 'I want you to find out everything you can about a man called Rodney Pertwee.'

Despite his ordeal, Scrivens was keen to return to duty. 'Wow!' DC Scrivens said. 'As in *the* Rodney Pertwee, sir?'

Angel blinked and said, 'Yes. The very same. Forensics and Dr Mac should have been informed. Check they are on their way.'

'Wow!' Scrivens said again. 'Right, sir.'

Angel closed his phone and looked around. 'Anybody seen the murder weapon . . . a gun of some sort?'

Schultz said, 'I have not seen any weapon, Inspector. I don't know if anybody else has.' He looked round the many faces near the sofa, watching and listening.

Lots shook their heads and some murmured 'No.'

Angel frowned. He didn't like the idea of a gun in the neighbourhood where nobody knew its whereabouts. The weapon usually turned up before the end of the enquiries. But

29

the sooner the better, before it was used again. Also it often gave some evidence that helped with the detection.

'Now where is the police photographer?' Angel said. Then he turned to Carter and said, 'In the absence of the SOCOs, Flora, I want you to take a photograph of the entire company on my mobile. You'll need to be a good distance away to get everybody in it.'

Carter took the phone, looked round the sound stage and made her mind up as to where she needed to be.

Angel then looked round for something to stand on. He found a chair and climbed onto it. Then he clapped his hands several times as loudly as he could manage and said, 'Can I have your attention, please, everybody? Thank you. Thank you.'

Eventually he caught everybody's attention.

'I am Detective Inspector Angel from Bromersley Police assigned to investigate the cause of Rodney Pertwee's death. It seems that he has been murdered. To find the murderer I need your cooperation. Would you all take up the exact place you were when the shots were fired. Please try and be accurate. I know the scene required very reduced lighting, but do your best, please. When you are in the correct position, please stand upright with your arms down by your sides. Thank you . . . Thank you . . . That's very good . . . Is that everybody? Yes, I believe it is. Good. Thank you. Now do you agree that the two people nearest to you are in the correct position?'

He looked around.

'If you think they are not, tell them. Please tell them.'

Everybody was still and silent.

'Everybody agrees that the two people nearest to them were in those positions the moment the gun was fired?'

There was no response.

'Thank you,' he continued. 'Now please hold your position while DS Carter photographs the scene.'

Angel dodged behind a scenery screen so that he wouldn't appear in the photographs. Carter quickly moved position slightly several times, pointing the camera at the cast and crew and tapping the screen of the mobile phone.

Then Carter called out, 'I've finished, sir.'

He waved an acknowledgement back to her, mounted the chair again and in a loud voice said, 'And my last question, as far as you know, is anyone missing now that was present at the time of the shooting?'

There was no response.

* * *

A few minutes later, the SOCOs arrived and the man in charge of them, Detective Sergeant Donald Taylor, dressed in white, rushed across to Angel.

'Man shot dead, Don,' Angel said. 'Body still in situ.'

'Right, sir. Where was the murderer standing when he fired the shot?'

'We don't know.'

Taylor's eyebrows went up.

Angel said, 'We'll rely on you to tell us.'

Angel looked for Schultz and said, 'Where is the lady who played opposite Rodney Pertwee?'

'Miss Rock, Samantha. She'll be in her caravan, I expect, Inspector,' Schultz said. 'It's the big white one.'

Angel knocked on the caravan door.

A beautiful young woman in street clothes, with a small pad of cotton wool in her hand, opened the door. She continued wiping make-up from her face.

31

'Are you the police?'

Angel introduced himself and DS Carter.

'Come in,' Samantha Rock said. 'Sit down. I can't tell you much. It's awful. We were holding each other at the time. I felt the vibration of the bullets go into him and then . . . his life drained away. I was only inches away from the bullets myself. It's something that has frightened me. I shall never get over it.'

Angel smiled sympathetically. 'You will, Miss Rock. You will. It is surprising what the human spirit can endure. Can you put up with some urgent questions at this time?'

'Oh yes. Of course.'

'Did Rodney Pertwee have any enemies? Was there anybody who would have wished him dead?'

'Oh no, Inspector. Not dead. I don't *know* of anybody, Inspector. He was extremely popular with national and international audiences. Tremendous box office success. I know that our director thought that Rodney Pertwee would pull this rather weak screenplay through to make the film a possible Oscar contender.'

'How did you get on with him?'

She hesitated. 'All right,' she said. 'He was a first-class actor.'

'I mean did you like him?'

'Not particularly. He was like so many men of his type. Made advances to every woman he fancied . . . thought his money, charm and good looks were the key to every woman's heart.'

'Did he make advances towards you?'

'Oh yes, but I was forewarned by Mr Schultz. Mind you, I was always polite, correct and professional. I reminded him — Mr Pertwee — that our relationship was entirely

32

professional and would be over in eight weeks' time anyway. Even so, he kept trying with invitations to extravagant restaurants in London and weekends in Paris.'

Angel nodded. 'Did he fear anybody?'

'I don't know, Inspector. I didn't know him that well. But I shouldn't think so.'

'Thank you, Miss Rock.'

When Angel and Carter were out of her caravan, Angel turned to Carter and said, 'While I remember, Flora . . . when we arrived at this place, and we came up to the front gate, I remember seeing a woman in a light-coloured raincoat and a green hat . . .'

'Yes. I remember her,' Flora said.

'I want to ask the man on the gate about her.'

'I've made a note, sir. Won't forget.'

SOCO had been very busy. The cast and crew who were standing around the sofa where the dead man lay, had been herded to one side of the stage and the area around the sofa had been taped off.

Angel saw Schultz heading to the caravan next to Samantha Rock's. Angel hailed him, 'Mr Schultz. I need to ask you some questions. Can we go somewhere to talk?'

'Of course,' he said, grabbing the door handle of his caravan. 'This is my office. Come in. Come in. Both of you,' he said, opening the door and gesturing to Flora to lead the way. 'I was coming here for a drink and a bit of peace. I have a bottle of whisky which we can share.'

'Not for us, Mr Schultz, but you carry on,' Angel said.

The German's bushy eyebrows shot up then he shrugged and said, 'Sit down, Miss. Sit down, Inspector.'

He went over to a cupboard and produced an unopened bottle of whisky. He put it on the desk in front of them.

Angel said, 'Tell me about Rodney Pertwee.'

Schultz's chins wobbled as he thought. 'Star actor. In the top three in the world. He was my first choice . . . you could say, the only choice of male lead in this film. I don't know where I can find another man who can give his all to the role. I keep thinking . . .'

Angel said, 'Did you like him?'

Schultz said, 'What's that got to do with it? As a matter of fact, I didn't care for him much. He was a woman's man, if you know what I mean. He knew what to say to women. He could charm them out of a tree. But to men, he was not so attractive.'

Angel nodded and said, 'Did he have a special lady friend?'

'Not that I know of, Inspector. But there were sometimes cars parked outside the main gate waiting for him to come out.'

Angel smiled a little, then shook his head and said, 'Are you staying in the UK for long?'

'I don't know. At least until this picture is put to bed. Losing our star will put us back a few weeks.'

Angel nodded sympathetically. 'Do you have family to consider? Your wife for instance?'

'There's nobody. I'm not married and my parents died a few years ago.'

'Where are you living while you are over here?'

'At the Feathers Hotel. I have a suite there.'

Angel looked at Flora. She wrote down the address and nodded.

'That'll be all for now, Mr Schultz,' Angel said.

* * *

At around that same time, Mrs Bridget Dalrymple knocked tentatively on the door of the two-room, seventh-floor, Leeds office of Mountjoy Productions.

A woman's voice called out, 'Come in.'

Nothing happened. There was another knock on the door.

'Come in! Come in!' she repeated.

The door handle slowly went down and the door was hesitatingly opened.

An Irish voice that sounded as if it had kissed the blarney stone many times said, 'Is this the office of Mr Mountjoy the film maker?'

'It is,' the young lady said. 'What can I do for you?'

The grey-haired figure in the green hat said, 'Glory be!' and closed the door. 'He didn't tell me it was up a mountain. I had to pretend to myself that I was walking up to the pearly gates of St Peter, or I would never have gotten here. If it had been downhill, I would not have taken a step.'

'You didn't *walk* up all those steps?'

'As true as my name is Bridget Dalrymple, every single one. And I know there is a lift. But they break down and I don't want to be a prisoner with strangers for hours on end. It's not healthy.'

The young woman smiled and said, 'Well, you're here now, Mrs Dalrymple. What can I do for you? I am Mr Mountjoy's assistant.'

'Now see, you've got me talking, Miss. I had nearly forgotten what I had come for. Will you please tell Mr Mountjoy, Bridget Dalrymple is here? He is expecting me.'

'I'm afraid Mr Mountjoy is not in, and I don't know when to expect him back.'

'Oh, Miss, that is terrible thing to say. I can't understand why he had forgotten I was coming . . . And I missed a special Mother's Union meeting to hear a priest from County Cork addressing us on his experiences with teenage girls and one-parent families, followed by afternoon tea and Mrs Doodle's special Battenburg cake.'

'I'm terribly sorry . . .'

Mrs Dalrymple's eyes and face showed she was at first disappointed, then her expression suddenly changed. It lit up. 'Well, I might be able to get back to the Church Hall to hear some of it. *And* still be in time for the tea.'

She opened the door and said, 'You'll be sure and tell Mr Mountjoy I called?'

'I certainly will,' the assistant said.

Bridget Dalrymple picked up her carrier bag and rushed out.

Peace and quiet resumed in the office for the next half an hour or so until the phone rang.

The secretary answered it briskly, 'Mountjoy Productions, can I help you?'

'Ah. Gloria, this is Edward Schultz. Can I speak to Maurice, please? It is extremely important.'

'This isn't Gloria, sir. She's left. I'm Isolde. And I am afraid that Mr Maurice is out.'

At that moment, the office door opened and Maurice Mountjoy rushed in.

Isolde said, 'Ah, sorry. He just walked in.' Then away from the phone, he heard her say, 'It's Mr Schultz and he wants to speak to you. Says it's important.'

Mountjoy nodded and with a finger gestured that he would take it in his office.

She came back to Schultz and said 'Mr Maurice has just come in. He'll be happy to speak to you in a few seconds when he reaches his desk. Would you please hold?'

'Thank you,' Schultz said. 'Tell him to please hurry.'

She heard Maurice pick up the phone and speak and then she returned her phone to its cradle.

Then from the adjoining office, she suddenly heard Mountjoy scream, '*What!*'

'It needn't cost much, Maurice,' Schultz's voice boomed over speaker phone. 'The opening scene lasting about three minutes will have to be shot again and the short piece we did today. That's all. There weren't any close-ups of Pertwee on a horse. He was terrified of horses. All the long shots and middle-distance shots were of a stand-in.'

'Are you sure?' Maurice said. 'Who do you want now? His name was the big attraction of the film. The box office.'

'Don't I *know* that? Get as big a name as you can get at such short notice. Box office name. Young. Handsome. Not every box office draw is in work. Depends on how much money he is looking for.'

'Who fired the gun, Edward? I assume it was one of the cast or someone in the crew. He will also have to be replaced.'

Schultz sighed. 'I don't know. You should come down here. We are in the hands of the police.'

'I'm on my way,' Mountjoy said.

He returned the phone to its cradle.

'Maria,' he called. 'No, erm, Gloria, I mean.'

'I assume you mean me,' Isolde called back and came into his office with notebook and pencil.

'Sorry,' he said. 'Yes, Isolde. Any messages?'

'Only an Irish woman, Mrs Bridget Dalrymple. She wants to see you. Said she had an appointment.'

Mountjoy's face creased with dismay. 'Oh yes,' he said. 'I'll deal with her later.'

He rushed off to the film studio.

FOUR

Maurice Mountjoy reached the film studio a worried man and buttonholed Angel and Carter as they were leaving the scene.

'Inspector Angel!' Mountjoy called out. 'I know that the murder of Rodney Pertwee is a terrible thing, and his family have my deepest sympathy, but I too now have a crisis on my hands. It leaves me with a whole list of problems, I can tell you. Not the least, I now have sixty-two people depending on me to stump up a salary every month for employment which is held up because we are a lead actor short and the sound stage has been closed. You can do nothing about us being a lead actor short, but you could open the sound stage.'

Angel had sympathy with him, but he did have a murder to solve. 'If our investigation goes well, I think it could be opened the day after tomorrow,' he said.

Producer Mountjoy pulled a disappointed face. 'That's more than half a week, Inspector.'

'That's the best I can say, Mr Mountjoy. If we find anything of interest, it could take longer.'

Mountjoy looked upwards. 'Oh no. I hope not.'

'While you are here,' Angel said, 'please tell me, where were you at eight forty-five this morning?'

'I was at home.'

'Were you alone?'

'Yes, I'm afraid I was.'

* * *

'My name is Ken King. They call me the sound boy, Inspector,' the man said. 'I suppose I should be flattered by the title considering I am sixty-two.'

Angel smiled politely then said, 'I understand you wanted to tell the investigating officer something very important about the murdered man, Rodney Pertwee.'

'Yes.'

'You knew him well?'

'No. Not at all, but you know, before he arrived on the set, we were unofficially told not to sit at the same table he may be at in the canteen. Not to try to start a conversation with him. Not to ride with him in the lift. Not to approach him for any reason. He thought he was more important than God.'

'This didn't apply to you only?'

'It applied to the crew and almost all the cast. He only wanted to mingle with the rich and famous.'

Angel rubbed his chin thoughtfully then said, 'Is that it?'

'I thought you should be told, because perhaps nobody else would tell you.'

'Thank you,' Angel said.

He thought that while it was interesting to know this aspect of the victim's psychology, it wasn't a motive to kill him.

'While you are here, I might as well ask you where you were at eight forty-five this morning?'

'Oh. I was there. I was standing next to Mr Lee, behind the camera. You have me on the photograph on your phone.'

* * *

Angel and Carter saw all the others who were on Sound Stage Two at the time of the shooting and asked preliminary questions. Nothing useful resulted from the interviews. Angel didn't see any leads. It would involve a lot more legwork if SOCO didn't come up with something scientific.

The day raced by as it does when there is a lot to do.

It was twenty to five and dark outside.

They went out of the sound stage and returned to Angel's car.

At the barrier, the man said, 'Did you find out who did it, sir?'

'Not yet. But we will. By the way, as we arrived earlier a woman in a green velvet hat—'

'That was Mrs Dalrymple,' he said quickly. 'Mrs Bridget Dalrymple. What about her?'

'Does she work here?'

'I believe she works in the canteen.'

'Have you her address?'

'The canteen manager will have it.'

Angel's facial expression showed he wasn't pleased.

The barrier man smiled. 'Don't worry, Inspector,' he said. 'I have his phone number. Do you want me to get him for you?'

Angel nodded.

A minute later Angel was talking to the canteen manager.

'I have nobody of that description on the canteen staff, nor anyone called Bridget Dalrymple,' he said. 'I should try HR.'

Angel spoke to the manager of Human Resources and received a similar reply.

He closed the phone thoughtfully, looked at Carter then at the man on the barrier and said, 'There's only you who has seen the woman and even knows her name. How do you explain that?'

The barrier man looked surprised. He shook his head and said, 'She's very talkative. I'm sure she said she worked in the canteen. I've told you all I know about her.'

'How often does she come through here?' Angel said.

'Not very often.'

'Next time you see her, ask her to come and see me. I am anxious to have a word or two with her.'

* * *

Early the following morning, Old Norman was up early from under his cardboard bed in the shelter of the back doorway of the Feathers Hotel. It was the important morning of the week for him. It was bin collection day in that area of the town and he didn't want to miss anything choice.

He began his rounds searching the wheelie bins nearest to him in the central quarter of the town around where he slept. He was hungry and cold so he approached the Feathers' bins hopefully. His grubby, mitten-covered fingers scrambled through the empty cartons, bags and packets with no positive results. He had once come across half a packet of Weetabix which, softened with rainwater, had been more than enough for a meal that morning.

Norman found some small flakes in the bottom of the bag in a box of cornflakes. There wasn't much but it was something. He rolled up the bag roughly and stuffed it into his pocket.

Out of the corner of his eye, he saw an objectionable face appear at a small window in the back wall of the hotel. It didn't look at all friendly. He would avoid eye to eye contact and hope they'd go away.

Old Norman considered that the loss of his wife, then his job, then his house, followed by a long illness and his subsequent alcoholism, earned him the right to take what was useful to him from items that those with too much had discarded.

He speeded up his searching and came upon some grease-proof paper with three butter pats on it. He folded the paper and pushed that into his pocket. They would be useful if he found any cake or bread. He came across last Sunday's unopened newspaper. He stuffed it down his coat front — he liked to keep abreast of what was happening in the world. He reached the bottom of the bin so he levelled it all down and moved onto the next bin.

Norman always insisted on being thorough because sometimes something very interesting turned up in the most unexpected waste bins.

He dived into the next bin with enthusiasm, although it seemed only to hold shredded paper, torn sheets from an accounts ledger and plastic drinking cups. However, suddenly he touched something metal, cold and heavy. It was a hand-gun. A Glock. His heart thumped hard and fast. He knew enough to know how to check if it was loaded or not. He released the magazine from inside the hand grip. He could see it had at least three rounds showing . . . fully loaded it would hold a lot more. He returned the magazine to the hand grip. Then, nonchalantly looked round to see if anybody was watching him. The unwelcome face at the small window had gone. It seemed safe. So he took out the gun and slipped it quickly into his overcoat pocket. Then he shuffled out of the ginnel to the corner. He put his hand in his right-hand trouser pocket and took out a few coins. He did a quick mental sum and then walked up the ginnel to the main road, turned right, walked two hundred metres to a red post office telephone box on the pavement. A minute later he was talking to the night duty sergeant at Bromersley Police Station.

'This is Norman here. I want to speak to Inspector Angel. It's extremely important.'

'He's not in yet, Norman. He usually starts at eight thirty. Can I help you?'

'It's a matter of great importance. Will you please give him a message? Tell him it was from Old Norman.'

* * *

Detective Inspector Michael Angel took a detour on his way to the police station that morning. He drove into Bromersley town centre, stopped the BMW across the ginnel to the back of the Feathers Hotel and lowered the nearside front window.

He didn't have to wait.

Old Norman's usual daytime resting place was on a thin pile of cardboard between two bins against the hotel wall. When he saw Angel's car stop, he rushed up the ginnel towards the car.

'What's the matter, Norman?'

The old man squeezed his head, a shoulder and an arm through the window.

'I've found this, Michael,' he replied, then he passed him the handgun roughly wrapped in newspaper. 'I found this on my morning rounds.'

43

Angel, mystified, took the bundle and began to open it on his lap.

Norman said, 'Don't let anybody here see what I've given you. It's loaded. So be careful.'

Angel's mouth dropped open as he saw the handgun and realised that Norman had not been exaggerating.

'I think these days, it's five years just for possession, isn't it?' Norman said. 'I thought you had better have it. You'll know best what to do.'

'How did you come by it?' Angel said.

'It was between some torn ledger sheets in a wheelie at the back here. I don't like having a thing like that about. Will you get rid of it?'

'Gladly. Good to get another weapon off the streets, Norman,' Angel said, dropping it into his pocket. 'I will want my lads to have a good look at it. Is there anything else?'

'Nothing else, Michael.'

Then Angel fumbled around with his wallet then pressed a folded a ten-pound note into a horny, rough hand. 'Thank you very much, Norman.'

The old man looked at it, beamed at him and said, 'You didn't have to do that.'

Angel smiled and patted him gently on the shoulder a couple of times.

Norman looked unblinking into Angel's eyes as he pulled himself out of the window and said, 'Take care.'

'I will. I will.'

* * *

Angel and Carter arrived at the station at six o'clock and returned to their respective offices. Angel found a small pile of

44

envelopes in an elastic band on his desk. He whisked through them to find those he thought the most urgent. They would usually be the handwritten ones.

There was one. It was addressed to him personally, which was unusual. It was postmarked Harrogate. He slit open the envelope and took out the letter. It was written by hand in block capital letters. It said:

I AM LOOKING OUT FOR YOU, ANGEL. I AM GOING TO KILL YOU. I'M GOING TO KILL YOU WHEN YOU LEAST EXPECT IT.

That was it. It was unsigned.

Angel's heart began to thump. He grimaced and turned the letter over. There was nothing on there. He checked for prints or indentations from earlier writing. Nothing.

He examined the envelope. The same.

He rammed the letter into the envelope and tossed it into the wastepaper basket.

He had received scores of anonymous, threatening letters over the years and here was another. They were usually connected to a case he had just finished or was still working on, but he had nothing currently happening associated with Harrogate.

He frowned.

Then he reached down into the wastepaper basket and pulled out the envelope. He opened it up and read it again. The writer had used the words 'kill you' twice as if he had needed to emphasise it.

Angel stroked his chin.

He tried to smooth the paper even more by rubbing his closed fist across it several times. After a few seconds, he folded it, put it in the envelope, opened the middle drawer of his desk and pushed it in there. He would come back to it, if need be.

However, he couldn't get the letter with the Harrogate postmark out of his mind. It was something else he had to worry about. Especially at night . . . it was November . . . and longer, darker nights were a villain's friend. In the early hours, every unidentifiable sound caused his heart to beat faster and his breathing to become erratic. Every bang, creak or thump . . .

FIVE

The following morning, there was a knock on Angel's office door. It opened and DS Taylor put his head in.

'Got a minute?' he said.

'What is it, Don?' Angel said.

The detective sergeant came in, closed the office door and said, 'It's about the gun found in the Feathers Hotel waste bin.'

He held up a beige folder.

Angel said, 'What have you got?'

'No prints on the gun. And so I passed it on to ballistics.'

'Right,' Angel said, looking thoughtful. 'Have you had their report?'

Taylor put the folder down on the desk. 'It's all in there, sir.'

'What does it say?'

Taylor picked up the folder, opened it and said, 'It says that they discovered that the Glock handgun found in the wheelie was part of a consignment bought by the Ministry of Defence and stolen in transport to the Catterick Army

Training Camp in 2009. Nothing known as to its whereabouts after that.'

Angel wrinkled his nose. 'That's not much help. What does it say about the Pertwee murder?'

Taylor said, 'It says that the two shots fired were from a .38 at an angle ranging between fifty-five and ninety degrees. The first shot would have killed the victim outright. There were no powder burns. That's all.'

Angel scratched his head and said, 'So the gunman would have been more than two metres away from the victim. Well, thank you for that, Don.'

'Right, sir,' Taylor said and went out.

Angel frowned, thinking. There were no leads from ballistics. It meant that all the cast and crew on the set — except Samantha Rock — were still possible suspects of the murder of Rodney Pertwee. That was about one out of fifty or so. Flora had a list of the names and was going through them . . . history, background . . . all that kind of stuff. He hoped she would have better luck.

Angel leaned further back in his swivel chair. He closed his eyes momentarily. He tried to think constructively about the murder of Rodney Pertwee. He needed a suspect or more than one . . . there wasn't enough evidence yet to convict a flea. The more he thought and concentrated on the very few facts to hand, the more the letter bearing the Harrogate postmark dominated his thought process — and there was no ignoring it for long.

His landline phone rang.

Angel opened his eyes, shook his head and reached out for the phone.

The caller began with a loud long cough. Angel knew it could only be his boss, Detective Superintendent Horace Harker.

'Angel here, sir.'

'Come on up here,' Harker said.

It was an unspoken arrangement that Harker was in charge of the running of the small police station and Angel was responsible for all the detection of crime.

Angel was mostly left alone to work with limited resources, being a small unit. Most of the time it worked very well.

Angel went up to the top of the corridor, knocked on the door and walked in.

Harker's office was as sweaty as a kitchen in a curry house in Kolkata. But unfortunately, it didn't smell of wonderful spices. It smelled of menthol, as always.

DS Harker himself was not immediately visible. He was seated at his desk behind several piles of letters, files, reports and books. Strewn all around him was an assortment of medications. In boring moments, Angel tried to read the labels of some of them. They were used to treat arthritis, headache, coughs and colds, upset stomach, gout . . . and various other complaints Angel could neither pronounce nor spell.

Harker's head was the shape of a turnip. He was mostly bald but had a collar of white hair.

'Sit down, Angel, and tell me — what's this I understand from your reports that a famous film star, Rodney Pertwee, has been murdered and that you are auditioning for the part? Are you trying to get into the film business by the back door?'

'No, sir,' Angel said, not surprised at the confusion but amazed at the jibe.

Angel laboriously explained the case to the superintendent and the steps he was taking to catch the murderer.

'You must not keep arresting people, putting the station to the cost and inconvenience of being run like a five-star hotel — fetching and carrying after prisoners. And the cost of overtime by PCs putting in extra hours every day as jailers.'

Angel wasn't pleased. He had heard it all before. But he hadn't the patience or time to argue the point. It was very irritating. If he had to arrest somebody who was guilty of a crime, he would arrest them.

'We have to consider the cost of this station to the government,' Harker said. 'Whatever we do, we have to consider the cost. If there is a cheaper way of doing it, we should do it.'

Angel turned away to conceal his irritation.

After a while he said, 'Yes, sir.'

He came out of Harker's office and saw a plastic cup on the corridor floor. He kicked it wildly and energetically all the way down the hall and up to his office door. He opened the door, bent down, retrieved the cup, hurled it strongly towards his wastepaper basket and slammed his office door.

He slumped down in the chair, looked at the notes on his desk and the beige folder containing information on the Glock gun.

Suddenly, the office door opened and a small figure of a man in a smart suit with a waistcoat peered in.

'Is it convenient, Michael?' he said.

Angel smiled. 'Of course it is. Come along in.'

It was Dr Mac, the local Home Office pathologist. He had a shock of white hair and carried a large black bag.

'It's always a pleasure to see you, Mac.'

Angel stood up and shook his hand.

'Can't stop, Michael. Late for an appointment.'

Then Mac opened the big bag, took out a thin file and said, 'Post-mortem report on Rodney Pertwee, hand delivered,' he said with a grin.

'Thank you, Mac,' Angel said. 'Anything unusual?'

'No. Two .38 bullets entered the skull. The man would be brain dead after the first.'

'Anything else?'

'Nothing else of interest . . . it's all in there,' he said, pointing at the file. 'Must go, Michael. Any queries give me a ring.'

'Will do,' Angel said.

And Mac was gone.

Angel read the post-mortem report. It contained standard information and seemed of little use in solving the murder.

There was a knock on the door and DS Carter looked in. 'I have discovered something of interest, sir,' she said, waving her notebook.

He closed the post-mortem file and tossed it onto his desk.

'I could do with a lead, Flora,' Angel said.

'It concerns Edward Schultz.'

'Tell me,' Angel said. 'Sit down.'

'Edward Schultz was born in Germany and has a chequered history. I have been talking to my opposite number in Germany. He said that Schultz wanted the big time. While he was at college he was pedalling drugs and went to jail for it. When he was released, he went to Hollywood as an actor. While he was there, he became a producer and borrowed an enormous amount of money to make films. He engaged leading actors, directors and crew at enormous expense to make three films. Sadly, all three failed. And he now owes an impossible amount of money. I suppose he's paid *some* off but . . .'

Carter shrugged.

Angel's mouth dropped open. He rubbed his chin. That history certainly made Schultz a suspect . . . an unlikely suspect but at last a name to put at the top of the list.

* * *

The church in the centre of Bromersley rang out the Westminster chime telling those interested that it was half past five.

Angel yawned.

It was the end of a frustrating day.

He closed the file he had been reading. It was background about Rodney Pertwee. He put it in the middle desk drawer and saw the edge of the envelope containing the anonymous letter.

He hesitated. The muscles round his mouth tightened, his nose wrinkled and the corners of his mouth turned downward.

He considered reading it again, then decided against it and quickly shut the drawer.

If absolutely necessary, he would fight any person or thing he could *see*, but it seemed that Mr Anonymous might appear anytime without declaring their identity, anywhere with any kind of weapon. And he would have to be prepared for any eventuality.

He put on his coat and trilby and made his way out through the rear door of the police station to his car. It was dark, but the car park was illuminated. He drove the BMW out onto the road and turned towards the ring road. Two hundred yards later, traffic lights caused him to stop. As he gently applied the brakes, a big car in the next lane on his right also glided to a stop. The driver took the opportunity to light up a half-smoked cigar. Angel casually glanced across in his direction. In the flickering light of the match, he instantly recognised the man. It was Edward Schultz.

Angel's pulse raced. He didn't know why. He wondered if he should follow him . . .

The lights changed to green and Schultz made his way ahead of Angel. For a mile or so Angel changed lanes and allowed a car to drop between them. He passed the turning he usually took for home and thought briefly about Mary who would be looking at the clock and impatiently tapping her foot.

Schultz carried straight on so Angel followed with the one car between them.

What Angel failed to notice was a large Ford car following him. It had been following him since before the ring road. It had large headlamps and a big, ugly driver with an enormous nose and matching ears.

Shortly afterwards Schultz switched on his left indicator.

Then Angel switched on his left indicator.

And the Ford car driver behind him switched on his left indicator.

As the three cars peeled off the ring road, and the Ford car's headlights swept across Angel's rear mirror, he became positive that he was being followed.

His heart began pounding louder. He licked his lips.

He saw a signpost. It said, ROYSTON 4. RYHILL 6.

He knew he was in the countryside between Barnsley and Bromersley. The place was pitch black. There were no streetlights or houses. The road was narrow and bumpy.

Angel continued following Schultz's car along this narrow, winding road, holding back quite a way, hoping he had not been sussed. There was a T-junction ahead. Schultz turned right. Angel came up to it. There was a road sign. It said left to Bromersley, right to Wakefield. Of course he followed Schultz. And of course, the Ford followed on.

Then, suddenly, Schultz's car increased in speed from a steady fifty to seventy-five. It was as if he had suddenly spotted that he was being followed.

Angel kept up with him but it was a wild journey along those narrow, winding roads at that speed. The spurt lasted about a minute.

Schultz quickly turned left with the squeal of the tyres on two wheels. Angel wasn't far behind him and then Angel saw something . . . a packet, he thought . . . came flying out of the nearside front window of Schultz's car.

Angel couldn't see exactly where it landed. It must have been on the path or on the grass verge. He noted it was by a telegraph pole next to a gate into a field.

After that, Schultz drove in a most proper, regular fashion through a village to the main road back to Bromersley followed by Angel who continued to be followed by the Ford.

Schultz arrived at the Feathers Hotel and drove straight into the underground car park. Angel knew that there was a lift there that would take him directly to the floor of his suite.

Angel drove onto the public car park in front of the hotel, and the man in the Ford drove to a space nearby.

Before the wheels of the Ford stopped turning, Angel was out of his car and at the side of the Ford. Then he yanked open the Ford driver's door, dragged the big man out of his seat and roughly pushed him against the side of the car, his belly button against the door handle and one arm up his back. Then Angel searched in his pocket for his handcuffs. But the man was too strong for him. The man turned round, and with his free hand grabbed Angel securely by the throat and tightened his grip.

Angel's face constricted with pain. He was angry. He battered the man's head with heavy blows until he had to release the grip on his throat. He pushed Angel away but Angel gave the big man a mighty punch on the chin. It caused him to stagger against the car. Angel then followed up with another blow. And he was ready to follow up with a third, when the man put up his open hands briefly, shook his head several times, then dropped to one knee.

Angel thought the man was surrendering but it was cover to reach into his jacket and pull out a pistol. He stood up and pointed it directly into Angel's face.

'Put your hands up,' the man said. 'What's your game? I am a police officer with Special Branch.' The man flashed his wallet to show his ID.

Angel blinked and said, 'I am an Inspector with Bromersley Police.'

* * *

Angel made a quick break with the Special Branch man. Neither man explained to the other what they were doing that had caused their paths to cross. And both of them were quick to leave the scene.

Angel knew Mary would be worrying. But he needed to recover that packet that Schultz had winged from his car before anybody else did. He thought if he left immediately he would have the best chance of finding it. It was only about four miles away.

He made straight away for Wakefield Road. He recalled the turnings as they appeared in his headlights and he soon arrived at the corner where Schultz had swung his car round on two wheels, then out of the dark emerged the telegraph pole and the gate into a field. He knew he was at the right place. He stopped his car, took a torch from the dashboard and got out. He flashed the torch along the grass verge systematically but he could not see the packet. Then he shone the torch up and down the hawthorn hedge. Perhaps the person for whom it was intended had recovered it. He was about to give up searching, and then he saw it, resting in the hedge. He pulled it out. It seemed heavy for its size. Delighted with his success, he ran back to the car, put the packet onto the seat beside him and made it back home to Mary as fast as the roads, the law and his ability as a driver could take him.

* * *

In his office the following morning, Angel told DS Taylor the events he had been involved with during the previous evening and concluded by saying, 'The Special Branch man doesn't know that I went back and found the packet, nor does anybody else. And I haven't had the opportunity to open the packet until now.'

Don Taylor said, 'You are not thinking it's a bomb, are you, sir?'

Angel's eyebrows shot up. 'No, I am not.'

He reached out for his briefcase, took the packet out and handed it to Taylor and said, 'And I thought it would be advisable to open it with somebody else present . . . somebody with scientific knowledge.'

The packet was neatly wrapped in brown paper fastened with brown adhesive paper tape. It was not labelled and there was no writing on the outside.

Taylor took the packet and immediately said, 'It's heavy . . . don't think it's explosive. Must weigh about a kilo.'

He laid the packet at the end of Angel's desk.

Angel moved the desk light and the telephone a little to make room for the packet.

'There might be fingerprints around where the tape is,' he said. 'I need a Stanley knife,' he said. He fumbled around the top pocket of his jacket and took out a plastic tube shielding a very sharp steel blade. With the blade he began to cut the brown paper round the edge of the packet. He cut round three edges then with tweezers he turned over the brown paper to reveal a polythene bag containing a white powder. He didn't pick it up. Angel and Taylor just looked down at the bag in silence. They were both momentarily horrified.

Eventually Taylor said, 'Heroin?'

'Looks like it. That's why Schultz threw it away. Possession is automatically prison. He was presumably in the process of delivering it. Didn't want to be caught holding the baby.'

* * *

Late that afternoon, Angel called in Carter and told her about the attack on his way home the previous day and said, 'Will you search the records and see if anything comes up for the name "Ferris"? I think it's a man's name, but I don't know.'

Then he picked up his trilby and turned to go when the landline phone rang. He reached out for it. It was the station receptionist. 'There's a man on the phone wanting to speak to you. He refuses to give his name, but he says he knows the whereabouts of the woman in the green hat. Will you speak to him?'

Angel's eyebrows shot up. 'Put him through,' he said.

'Go ahead, Inspector.'

'Angel here, who is that?'

'I read in the paper that you are looking for an Irish woman, wearing a light raincoat, a green hat and carrying a carrier bag.'

Angel couldn't discern much from the voice. All he could be sure of was that it was local and mature.

'Yes,' Angel said.

'I have seen a woman of that description go into Saint Patrick's Church on Regent Street.'

Angel knew the place. It was the most prominent Roman Catholic Church in the town and was located in the town centre.

His pulse beat a little faster. 'When was this?'

'About ten minutes ago.'

Angel's mouth went dry. All his senses were heightened. He needed to catch that woman.

'Thank you,' he said. 'And what is your name?'

The line went dead. Angel's bottom lip tightened back across his teeth. He slammed the receiver back into its cradle, snatched up his hat, switched out the light and ran along the corridor out through the rear door to his car. He broke all speed limits and was there in Regent Street, outside the church, several minutes later. The stained-glass windows were illuminated by candlelight and showed bible characters and scenes. Angel parked on the road outside the front door of the church and rushed into the porch. He removed his hat and opened the door. The altar was beautiful and brilliantly illuminated. The rest of the building was in darkness.

He looked around and no one was to be seen.

Angel stood at the back for a few moments, overwhelmed by the magnificence of the altar and the quiet and stillness of the building. And then he saw that something was happening at the front of the church. Somebody was there and they were standing up. A head and body in silhouette rose up and made a quick exit through the door into the vestry.

It was Bridget Dalrymple.

Angel ran down the aisle and across the front of the altar to the side to the vestry door. He yanked it open to find the vestry in darkness. He couldn't see an inch in front of him. He felt around the wall near the door for a light switch. Nothing. He held his hands up in front of him and took small steps straight ahead in the darkness. Then he felt a wave of cold air on his face. A door to the outside winter evening had been opened. He heard running footsteps . . . away from him . . . more than one set . . . he shuffled in that direction and then saw the welcome light of the sky through an open door. He ran towards the outside door and through it. He saw a short footpath straight ahead, leading to a T-junction. To the right seemed to lead through gravestones to the presbytery, and to the left straight into Regent Street.

He glanced up and down Regent Street and in the street lighting none of the few pedestrians about resembled Bridget Dalrymple. He stood silently against the side of the church and listened and watched for five minutes. Nothing moved. It was dark but there was enough light not to walk into gravestones. He took the path to the presbytery . . . a few steps. He found the front door and pressed the bell.

A young priest came to the door. 'Can I help you?'

Angel held up his warrant card and badge. 'I am a police inspector, Father, and I am looking for an Irish woman, Mrs Bridget Dalrymple, medium build in a green hat. Can you help me? Have you seen her?'

The priest shook his head. 'No, I don't think I know her, Inspector. I'm sorry.'

'Well, I'm sorry to have troubled you, sir,' Angel said. 'I'll say goodnight.'

'Goodnight.'

Angel, not surprised but nevertheless disappointed, turned away from the big, dark presbytery into the gloom.

The many gravestones around the church provided excellent hiding places so he began looking among them. The woman couldn't disappear. He walked up a lane of bigger memorial gravestone decorations . . . angels and cherubs on each side.

Suddenly, Bridget Dalrymple appeared from behind a marble-like angel, pointing a handgun at Angel's stomach and said, 'Glory be! But you must be that Inspector Angel that's making a nuisance of himself.'

Angel looked composed on the surface, but seeing the glint of the handgun pointed at him, his senses underneath were feverishly working to find a way to reverse the situation.

'Bridget Dalrymple!' he said. 'Stay just where you are. You are under arrest for various charges including the murder of Rodney Pertwee. You do not have to say anything, but it may harm your defence . . .'

Bridget Dalrymple interrupted him saying, 'You needn't go through all that blether, Inspector. I don't mind admitting that I was glad when I heard of the demise of Rodney Pertwee. Nobody liked him. He was a servant of Satan. He was everybody's enemy . . . especially young Catholic girls. I reckon I did the Lord a service.'

Angel said, 'I don't want to take the Lord's name further in vain, Mrs Dalrymple, but however you look at it, you have committed murder and you have to pay for it.'

'I had hoped that we might get on a better footing together, and that we might come to an agreement.'

Angel said, 'What have you in mind?'

'How does five thousand English pounds in cash sound?'

'It sounds perfectly wonderful . . . and ten thousand English pounds in cash sounds even better.'

'Blest be the Saints!' Dalrymple called out.

Angel's face hardened. He said, 'You needn't put yourself out. I wouldn't accept a single penny of your drug money.'

Mrs Dalrymple shook the gun in her hand. 'You're making it mightily easy, Inspector, for me to pull this trigger.'

Angel's brain raced to find something to stop her . . . but he couldn't think of anything . . .

Suddenly, there was the sound of a door slamming. It was the presbytery door followed by quick footsteps.

At the same time, Angel heard a rustle of clothing from behind.

Mrs Dalrymple urgently said, 'Somebody coming. Let's go!'

Angel turned to receive a mighty blow to his temple from something hard and heavy which closed his eyes and sent him to the ground. He saw a bright white light for a few seconds. That went out and there was nothing but blackness.

His body hit the stone-flagged path and he lay there face down, an untidy, unconscious bundle.

A few moments passed.

Then, as Angel's head cleared, he heard a voice.

'Oh dear. I'm coming, sir. What's happened? Did you fall? You'll be all right. Shall I ring for an ambulance?'

Then much louder, the voice said, 'What's the matter? Are you ill?'

Angel felt an uncertain pair of hands turning him over. He could now see it was the young priest he had been talking to earlier.

'Thank you,' he said. 'Thank you very much.'

He sat up and looked round. Mrs Dalrymple had gone.

'Thank you,' Angel repeated. The movement of his head prompted him to touch a particular place. He felt a lump at the side of his head. His lips tightened momentarily. Apart from that he felt fine.

'You must have hit your head when you fell.' The young priest helped Angel to his feet.

'Yes,' Angel said. But he knew better.

SIX

It was early that Wednesday morning . . .

There was a knock on Angel's office door.

It was DS Carter. 'I've found something interesting. Is it convenient?'

'Of course, Flora,' Angel said from his desk. 'Come in. Sit down.'

'The film's cameraman, sir,' Carter said. 'James Lee. He is a suspect?'

'Definitely, Flora,' Angel said. 'He was about three metres away from Pertwee when he was murdered. What about him?'

'He told me that he has rented a house for his wife and daughter for the period of the making of the film from Webb's Estates.'

Angel screwed up his face. 'What's wrong with that?'

'The house he has rented is more like an estate. It's Tingle Hall.'

Tingle Hall was the biggest and most imposing living accommodation and gardens in Bromersley. After Lady Tingle died, it had been on sale for about ten years but there had been no buyers. Therefore, the new owner had taken to leasing it.

Angel's jaw dropped and he shook his head in surprise.

'I thought you'd be surprised,' Carter said.

Angel stood up. 'I know Tony Webb. Went to school with him. I'll go to Webb's and ask a few questions, Flora. I thought only kings and princes could afford to live in a place like that.'

'Right, sir,' she said and went out of the office.

Angel followed her moments later and made his way to his car. He was there in a few minutes. As he pulled up on King Street outside Webb's office, he saw Tony Webb leaning a signboard on the pavement outside his office, adding it to four or five others. They were all advertising property for sale or rent and forthcoming auctions.

As he got out of the car he said, 'Hello, Tony. Can I have a few words?'

'Hello, Michael. Of course. Come inside.'

He followed Webb through the front shop door, round the back of the reception counter along a short corridor, through a door into a small office.

There were files and letters all over his desk.

'Sit down, Michael,' Webb said. 'Excuse the mess. It's the year end and my help is off with flu.'

'Won't keep you long,' Angel said. 'You've a property on your books, Tingle Hall?'

Webb nodded.

'I understand that a Mr James Lee is renting the property for his wife, self and daughter?' Angel said.

Webb said, 'That's right.'

The shop doorbell rang out.

'Oh dear. Excuse me, Michael,' Webb said. 'I must answer it.' He stood up. 'Please wait. I won't be long.'

He opened the office door, left it open and went out to the front counter.

Angel sat there and glanced across the desk at the various piles of letters, ledgers and invoices. Nearest to him was a stack of files with names typed on the edge. Most of them were unfamiliar to him. But he did see one. It was titled, SCHULTZ, E. He frowned. He wondered what business Schultz had with Webb.

He looked across at the open office door . . . he could hear Webb and the other man still talking at the counter. The Schultz file was about halfway down. It could be in some sort of sequence. He quickly pulled it out but left the top half of the pile on the cross so that he would know where to replace it. Then he whisked open the file. It referred to a property in Scarborough owned by Edward Schultz and leased out by him through Tony Webb.

Angel suddenly heard the shop bell go.

His heart began to thump. He must remember the address . . . Mermaid House, Ocean Drive, Pilsboro, Scarborough.

The conversation had stopped. The visitor had gone.

Angel closed the file.

He slipped the file back in the pile and slammed the others on top as Webb appeared through the doorway.

Webb said, 'Sorry about that. It's what it's like when the help is off sick.' He sat at his desk and said, 'Now, where were we?'

'Tingle Hall,' Angel said. 'I was getting round to asking how a cinematographer such as Jimmy Lee can afford to lease Tingle Hall for eight or ten weeks?'

'Well, I believe that he has brought his wife and daughter . . . consider the cost of three of them in a hotel for eight weeks. And Jimmy Lee isn't any old cinematographer. He's in the top three in the business. He'll be earning a very good screw.'

* * *

Angel's desk phone rang out. It was Detective Superintendent Harker. 'Angel, come up to my office *now!*' he bawled and slammed down the phone.

Angel pulled an unhappy face. It was obvious trouble. He wondered what had disturbed the sleepy monster.

He made his way through the station, up the corridor, and knocked on the super's door.

'Come in,' Harker called.

Angel went into the menthol-laden greenhouse.

Harker was in uniform, seated at his desk, with a very smart man in plain clothes seated opposite him.

The superintendent pointed to a chair and said, 'Sit there, Angel. This is Commissioner Prentice from Special Branch.'

Prentice looked at him and said, 'Detective Inspector Angel, I just want to apologise for any inconvenience caused by Special Branch by the cross-following of a suspect late yesterday afternoon. It happens occasionally . . . rarely, I am pleased to say.'

Angel nodded and said, 'And I also apologise for any inconvenience I may have caused last evening, sir, but of course I had not been told in advance that you were operating in this area.'

Prentice shuffled uneasily in his chair and said, 'Ah well, we had no idea that we would be. We try always to inform our friends in the other services serving the public where we know in advance. By the way, Inspector,' Prentice said, 'as a matter of interest, what exactly were you doing last evening?'

Angel said, 'Well, on my way home in the car, I spotted a suspect in a case I was investigating. So I followed him to see what he was up to. What is the man to you, sir?'

'Simply a suspect we are also casing. I would be grateful if you said nothing of Special Branch to him or anyone else.'

'Of course. Of course, Commissioner,' Angel said. 'What was your interest in having the man followed?'

Prentice breathed in heavily. Angel's questions weren't welcome and the Inspector's answers to his questions weren't very informative.

'He is a cog in a large machine we are endeavouring to close down,' he said. 'Did the man — we are talking about Edward Schultz, I presume — did he go straight back to his hotel?'

'That's the man. Edward Schultz. What do you suspect him of doing?'

Prentice's fists tightened. His voice went up ten decibels as he said, 'Inspector Angel, don't you ever answer questions?'

Angel smiled and said, 'I notice you are not answering any questions I am asking. You must understand that I am chasing a murderer and Schultz is a suspect. I need to find out as much as I can about the man that is relevant. I will willingly tell you all I know about him if you will help me by reciprocating.'

Prentice rubbed his chin very hard. 'Very well, Angel. Let me see . . . a large shipment of Class A drugs is on its way by a small boat from South America. It is worth millions of US dollars. The boat is expected to dock in Ireland . . . the drugs will then be transported overland to make their way into Northern Ireland . . . and over the water to England, but we don't know where or when. When we are certain of the identity of the boat, we shall permit it to enter UK waters

— within twelve miles of our shores — and monitor its journey at a discreet distance to find all the personnel at its destination and arrest them. We also believe that it is being partly financed by Edward Schultz but we cannot prove it.'

Prentice paused, thought through what he had just reported then said, 'Yes. I think that's everything. Now, Angel, it's your turn.'

Angel nodded. 'Yes and thank you for that, sir,' he said. He cleared his throat. 'A young man was very recently murdered,' he began. 'And I have the responsibility of finding the murderer.'

He then related what happened that evening in some detail concluding with the following . . .

'And if you have a large-scale map, I will show you exactly where Schultz threw it. The packet of heroin with all the wrapping is here, with our SOC officer. You can see it now and take it with you, if you wish.'

Prentice rubbed his chin. 'Thank you, Angel,' he said, then pointedly looking at Harker, he added, 'Seems to me you have done a good, solid job.'

Harker sniffed and he must have thought that it was his turn to say something complimentary. He looked at Angel, wrinkled his nose and said, 'Yes. Well done, Inspector. Well done.'

* * *

Later that morning, Angel was in his office mulling over recent events, and it occurred to him that as Schultz had been in the drugs trade and that he owned Mermaid House on the coast, it was a possibility — no stronger than that — that the drugs reported to be on the way in a small boat from South America were to be delivered there. It was a good reason why Mermaid House should be kept under observation. He was anxious to see for himself what the house was all about.

There was a knock on the door.

'Come in,' Angel called.

It was Detective Constable Scrivens. He was holding an envelope. 'You wanted me, sir?'

'Yes, Ted.'

'This has come for you, sir,' Scrivens said, handing him the envelope. 'Second post.'

'Sit down,' Angel said.

The envelope was addressed to him personally, as before. It was handwritten in block letters. When he saw it was date stamped Harrogate his jaw tightened. He opened it carefully. It was written by hand in block capital letters.

It said:

I AM STILL LOOKING OUT FOR YOU, ANGEL. I MISSED YOU LAST WEEKEND. BUT I AM STILL GOING TO KILL YOU WHEN YOU LEAST EXPECT IT.

That was it. It was unsigned.

Angel sighed, pulled a face and turned the letter over. There was nothing on the other side. He checked for prints or indentations from earlier writing. Nothing.

He had received hundreds of anonymous, threatening letters over the years . . . and here were two more . . . from the same source. He dropped it on his desk breathed in and out deeply.

Much as he wanted, he couldn't get those two particular letters out of his mind. He couldn't recall meeting anyone in particular last weekend.

He picked it up and read it again. He examined the envelope.

After a few seconds, he opened the middle drawer of his desk and pushed it in there with the other one. He would come back to them when necessary.

'Anything wrong, sir?' Scrivens said.

Angel looked at him and said, 'Yes. Plenty.'

Then he remembered that he had summoned Scrivens there to ask him to do a particular job.

'Listen up, Ted. The cinematographer working on the film Schultz is directing is Jimmy Lee. Apparently greatly talented. His origins are Chinese or Asian. See what you can find out about him. See if he goes anywhere. See who his contacts are. He has his family with him. They are staying at Tingle Hall.'

'Tingle Hall?' Scrivens said. 'Yes, right, sir.'

Angel looked at him.

'Wow!' Scrivens said then rushed off.

Angel smiled when he considered that Ted Scrivens was so overawed by celebrities.

Angel then tidied his desk, put on his hat and coat and went past the cells to the rear door of the station and went out to the police car park. He started his car, set his Sat Nav to the post code for Schultz's property in Scarborough and then released the handbrake.

* * *

Edward Schultz sniffed unhappily at the chemical smell of fresh paint and signs around the floor reading WET PAINT as he reached the offices of Mountjoy Productions on the sixth floor of the office block in Leeds. He pressed down the door handle and walked in.

Isolde said, 'Good morning, Mr Schultz . . . what a pleasant surprise to see you. Oh dear. You'll be wanting to see Mr Mountjoy.'

Schultz's eyes flashed. 'I have an appointment with him. Is he not here *again*?'

Isolde's cheeks flushed up red. She put her head down in her desk diary. 'I haven't got a note of it. I can't think what's happened.'

Schultz stamped his feet then said, 'I will wait a very few minutes, but then I will go.'

'I am terribly sorry. Can I get you a cup of coffee or tea?'

'No thank you.'

Meanwhile, Bridget Dalrymple reached the top step of the sixth floor in the same office block carrying her brown carrier bag.

Her face was red and perspiring.

There were several signs around advising visitors of the wet paint on the walls and doors. A man in white overalls was busy with a paint roller. Bridget sniffed as she recognised the smell.

As Bridget caught her breath, the door of Mountjoy Productions opened and out came Edward Schultz. He went straight over to the lift and pressed the call button. At the same moment, the painter returned his paint roller to the paint tray, walked across to the lift door and stood next to him. Bridget Dalrymple moved swiftly to the lift door and stood on the other side of Schultz.

The lift doors opened but instead of the normal illuminated little cabin, the lift cage was not there and in the dark all that could be seen were cables and ropes disappearing down the lift shaft.

The painter and Bridget each grabbed an arm of Edward Schultz and pushed him over the edge into the lift shaft.

'Noooooo,' Schultz screamed.

But it was too late. Schultz lost his balance and dropped like a rag doll down the shaft, screaming as he went.

There was a dull thud, when he landed on the top of the steel cage.

SEVEN

It was 3.30 p.m. when Angel arrived at Pilsboro a few miles along the coast from Scarborough. There was very little traffic about — several delivery vans and a couple of cars all the way from York. It was still daylight, but the sky was as dull as a political speech.

It was easy to find Mermaid House. It was a large, solitary, white-painted detached house built on cliffs on the seafront. A narrow road ran down to the front of the house but only a footpath led to the rear entrance.

Angel drove the BMW down the road to the house but didn't hang about. He didn't want to be seen.

He saw that the house also had features on three sides. There was a garage for several cars, a swimming pool and plenty of areas for sheltered sunbathing. There was a smart, new-looking, luxury silver car standing on the drive. However, there were no signs of life. All the windows were closed, there was no washing out at the back and he couldn't see any electric light illuminating any of the rooms at the front.

He quickly turned the car round and came back out.

He was hungry. Pilsboro had no shops, so he went into Scarborough, found a supermarket where he quickly bought a sandwich and a bottle of milk. He returned to Pilsboro and then stopped the car on the promenade just as his mobile began to ring.

It was DS Carter ringing from the station.

'Are you all right, Flora?'

'It's four o'clock, sir. I'm ready for home . . . I haven't seen you all day. Thought I would check in with you. Have you heard the news?'

'What news?' Angel said.

'Edward Schultz was found dead in a lift shaft about an hour ago. Leeds CID reckon it's an accident.'

Angel's jaw dropped. He was suddenly very cold at the core. It spread throughout his body.

After a moment, he shook his head. He was thinking Schultz had been playing a dangerous game.

'I'm at his place just now, Flora. I guess it tracks that there's no one home . . . Weren't there any witnesses to tell us what happened?' he said.

'No. But that Irish woman, Bridget Dalrymple, and a painter were seen leaving the building.'

He cringed when he heard the name Bridget Dalrymple. He knew then that it couldn't possibly be an accident.

Angel said, 'If it is ever your bad luck to come into the presence of that woman, drop what you are doing, follow her and report to me where you are.'

'Right, sir.'

He ended the call, pocketed his mobile and got out of the car. The wind was biting his ears. He turned up his coat collar, leaned on the steel railings and looked out to sea . . .

then down to Mermaid House. He had a magnificent view of both the front entrance and the side door. He noticed that one of the front ground-floor rooms now had lights on, although the curtains were still closed. Then he looked along the promenade just below where he was standing and saw a small car park for about six cars. His cold, red face brightened . . . a wonderful place for him to be overlooking Mermaid House under the pretext of looking out to sea.

He found the entrance off the promenade to the little car park. It had a notice board supported by two tubular steel posts cemented into the ground. The board was painted with rules and regulations to users of the park and the costs in season.

Angel parked the BMW facing the sea . . . with a great observation point to view the big house.

It was twenty minutes to five and daylight had gone. The sky was filled with dark clouds and the moon wasn't showing her face.

His stomach told him it was an opportune time to have his sandwiches.

As he chewed away at the chicken sandwich in the dark, he heard the chug-chug sound of an engine. He opened the car window a little to hear it more clearly. Icy cold air blew strongly through the gap. He closed it quickly and reached out to the dashboard for the night binoculars. He looked out to sea. It was black and the horizon dissolved into cloud and fog. Angel followed the indistinct line from east to west and back again and saw nothing.

He lowered the binoculars.

The chug-chug noise was getting louder.

He lifted the binoculars again and saw a tiny grey spot making its way through the darkness. He continued to watch it. The spot began to take the shape of a boat . . . a small craft. It was making for Mermaid House and it was travelling without lights.

Fifteen minutes later, it chugged directly to some rocks at the side of Mermaid House. Angel saw only two men in yellow storm-proof coats with hoods on the deck of the small boat.

Then the boat went out of Angel's vision and the chugging sound stopped. He reckoned that it must have entered a cave that probably provided an entrance to the house.

Angel lowered the binoculars. He licked his bottom lip thoughtfully. At that moment, he would give a month's salary to see where the boat was moored and the reason for the visit.

Then he observed a car pulling up on the road in front of Mermaid House. In the next three minutes, six more cars and small vans arrived to form a short queue. The drivers remained in their vehicles.

At exactly five o'clock, the outside light was switched on, illuminating the front door and its surrounds, and the expensive car on the drive.

Angel stopped chewing. He licked his lips then wiped his hands and mouth on his handkerchief. He quickly picked up the binoculars and focused them on the front door.

The driver of the first car to arrive got out of his vehicle. He was a big man in his middle years wearing a T-shirt, jeans and trainers. He had a heavy tan and tattoos on his arms and neck.

He went through the gate, up to the front door and pressed the bell push.

It was promptly opened — and the man stepped inside without any introduction or ceremony — and then it was quickly closed.

Angel deduced that the visitor to the house must be known. His heart beat a little faster.

He focused the binoculars across the scene and he saw something hanging from one of the mirrors on the luxury car on the drive. It fluttered in the powerful breeze. Eventually he was able to make out what it said. Simply the one word: *OFFERS?* He wondered, was the car really for sale?

Two minutes later, the door opened again, the first visitor came out and the second in the queue went in.

Angel watched several more visitors enter and leave.

There were other cars, small vans, cyclists, as well as pedestrians arriving and joining the queue.

The queue got longer, then shorter, then longer again.

Angel rubbed his chin. He made a decision. He took out his mobile phone and tapped in a Wakefield number. He summoned the Armed Response Unit and spoke to the DI Waldo White who was on duty that day. Angel told him the situation and White said he would commit two units and himself to the operation and that they would be with him within the hour.

It pleased Angel because he knew Waldo and had worked with him on several occasions before. They arranged to meet on the coast road a mile or so out of Pilsboro.

Angel closed and pocketed the phone and reached out for the last sandwich, when there was a tap several times on the driver's window. He peered through the wet glass and the darkness to the outline of a man's face. He looked like a tramp, and seemed to be waving a cigarette around. Angel pressed the button to wind the window down.

The man put his hand on the car window ledge and waving the cigarette in the other hand said, 'Got a light, mister?'

Angel was not much impressed with the man. He needed a shave. And a bath. He smelled of cheap whisky.

His fingernails needed cutting. And he should go on a diet for a couple of years. Nevertheless, Angel pressed the BMW's cigarette lighter under the dashboard to the charge position.

'Yes,' Angel said.

'Stranger round here?' the man said.

Angel wrinkled up his face in order to see the man better in the limited light. 'Could be,' he said.

'Sure it's not to nosey around?' he said, nodding towards Mermaid House. 'You won't see much in this light.'

Angel heard the cigarette lighter click. It had reached maximum heat so it switched itself off.

Still holding onto the top of the lowered window with one hand, the man produced a gun in his other hand and pointing it at Angel's stomach said, 'Get out of the car.'

Angel leaned forward as if to begin to get out of the car, surreptitiously snatched the hot cigarette lighter from its holder, and stamped it hard on the back of the man's hand on the door while at the same time, with his free hand diving for the barrel of the gun diverting it away from his stomach and trying to take possession.

'Bloody hell!' the man yelled and managed to pull his hand away.

The gun fired and the bullet went into the fabric of the front nearside door.

In the tussle that followed, the gun dropped onto the ground.

The man kicked it and it went three metres or so away from the car. Then as the man went to retrieve it, Angel got out of the car.

Angel could see the outline of the man pointing the gun at him.

'Hold it, mister,' the man said. 'I've got you well in my sights. One more smart move like that and I promise you, you'll be dead.'

'What do you want with me?' Angel said.

'The boss don't want no snoopers. And no cops.'

The big man rubbed the back of his hand. His face indicated the pain of burning flesh. Angel saw him and enjoyed some satisfaction. The scuffle had not all been failure.

'Put your hands up, turn round and make your way down that path,' the man said. 'No funny business. I'll not hesitate to pull this trigger.'

Angel could see that it was the way from the little car park to the rear entrance of Mermaid House. The path consisted of about three hundred metres of rough steps cut into the rock and a hundred metres of crazy paving leading up to the back gate.

He made up his mind not to make any attempt to escape until he had seen inside Mermaid House. He was determined to get as much information as he could before the ARU arrived.

They soon reached the back gate of the house.

The big man said, 'Press the sneck. Open the gate. Go on through.'

They went up the short path to the back door.

'Knock on the door,' the man said.

A voice from inside said, 'Who is it?'

'Kelly.'

The door was unlocked and opened ten centimetres. An eye and a nose became visible.

The man said, 'Come on, Blondie. I've got a prisoner. Let us in.'

Slowly, the rest of the man became visible. He was a tall, heavy man with a lot of blond hair.

'He was up on Skye car park spying down here on us.'

They went inside the kitchen area. Angel looked round and found that everything was smart and clean.

Blondie looked Angel over and said, 'Who is he?'

Kelly said, 'That's what I want to know.'

Blondie frowned.

'Will you hold your gun on him while I search him?' Kelly said. 'Be ever so careful. He's too smart for his own good.'

After the pat down, Kelly took possession of Angel's wallet, ID and badge and mobile phone.

When he saw the badge and ID he gasped and said, 'He's a copper! Would you believe it. He's a bleeding inspector.'

Blondie looked at Kelly, then at Angel, speechless.

Kelly put the wallet, ID and badge back into Angel's pockets. The mobile phone he dropped on to the tiled kitchen floor and stepped upon it hard with the full weight of his body then he stabbed it several times with the heel of his boot.

Then Kelly pointed his gun at Angel, nodding at Blondie who put his gun back in his waist band.

'Must tell Foster,' Kelly said.

Then he pushed Angel out of the kitchen into a magnificent hall with wall lights and a huge chandelier with many glittering glass drops and other glass decorations. The centre piece was a wide staircase to the upper floor. On the ground floor were five painted, gilded and beautifully decorated doors.

Kelly knocked on one of the doors.

'Wait a minute,' a voice said.

The owner of the voice was Charles Foster. He was in another expensively appointed reception room.

Foster was a small man in striped, black-and-grey trousers, black coat and white shirt standing at a table he was using as a desk. He was counting a handful of bank notes. Standing next to him was a youth with a blank expression, long hair and in need of a wash and a shave.

Foster finished counting the notes and then looked at the youth and nodded. Then he handed the youth a plastic bag containing a small amount of white powder. The youth quickly stuffed it into his pocket and made for the door to the hall.

Blondie appeared, directed the youth out, then closed the front door and locked it.

Meanwhile, Foster made an entry in a book, then leaned forward, stretched his arm under the table and dropped the bank notes through the swivel lid of a green plastic waste bin especially appropriated for the job.

Then he called, 'Come in.'

Kelly jabbed Angel in his back with his gun through the door into the room.

Angel looked round the room. He eyed Foster closely to see if he knew him. He had no recollection that he did, and the name was not familiar.

Foster's eyebrows shot up. His lips tightened. He leaped out of the chair.

'Who is this?' he said.

Kelly said, 'He's a cop, Mr Foster.'

'A cop?' Foster said his eyes flashing angrily. 'A policeman?'

'Yes. He was spying down on us from Skye car park.'

Foster's face was scarlet. He glared at Kelly.

'You blundering fool. You bring him here? Of all the places in the world you could have taken him you bring him to the one place where you *shouldn't* have. You idiot.'

'Well, what do you want me to do with him?'

'There's only one thing we *can* do with him now. And that is up to you, so get on with it. That's what you are paid for. And don't do it in the house. Take him well away from here.'

A shaft of ice ran down Angel's spine and spread across his body, settling at his stomach.

Kelly stood there with his eyes glazed.

Foster said, 'Now, get along with you. You couldn't have bothered me at a worse time. You can see how busy I am. Just when we have a big delivery. And there is a queue. Don't bother me anymore. You know what to do. *Get on with it.*'

Kelly looked at the floor. 'What else could I have done?'

Foster said, 'I don't know, Kelly, and I don't care. Get out and take that policeman with you.'

Kelly hesitated. He was still considering what to reply.

'You are holding me up,' Foster said and directed Kelly towards the open door.

Blondie appeared at the door. 'Ready for the next punter, Mr Foster?'

'I will be when Kelly and this policeman are out of my sight.'

Blondie winked at Kelly and said, 'Come on, Kelly. Whatever it is we can settle it later. At the moment there is a queue outside and somebody might notice.'

Kelly gritted his teeth. He jabbed the gun in Angel's back and said, 'Come on, copper. Let's go.'

He directed Angel across the hall and into the kitchen.

Angel knew that once he left the area around the house Kelly would certainly pull the trigger and kill him. Angel had purposely acted docile and made no attempt at taking the gun from Kelly so that he would naturally become slack and — hopefully — take the odd risk. When he did, Angel would be ready to take maximum advantage.

Kelly took Angel up to the back door. The key was in the lock.

'Open it up, Angel,' he said, waving the gun at him.

Angel had noticed that Kelly always held the gun in his right hand.

It was at that moment that Angel had an idea. He turned the key quite correctly in an anti-clockwise direction which unlocked the door. Then he put his hand on the doorknob and deliberately put his foot at the bottom of the door and attempted to pull the door open by turning and pulling. He made several pointless tries.

'It won't open. It's stuck,' Angel insisted slyly.

'Try it again,' Kelly said, waving the gun around. 'We've had no trouble with it.'

Angel continued to fool the man with the gun. He locked the door again and made several more fruitless tries at opening it.

Kelly ran his hand through his hair several times and said, 'Come out of the way, Angel. Let me have a look at it.'

Kelly changed places with Angel. 'Stand over there,' he said to him, still holding the gun in his right hand.

Angel had deliberately left the door locked.

Kelly attempted to open it by pulling and turning the doorknob with his left hand. It didn't open. He tried to open it again. He thought a moment. Then he put the gun in his left hand.

Angel's pulse raced. It was what he had been waiting for him to do. Then Kelly turned and pulled the doorknob with his other hand.

Angel promptly — with both of his hands free — leaped on the gun.

There was a bit of a struggle but Angel took the gun from him easily.

Kelly glared at him and said, *You bastard!*'

Holding the gun confidently, Angel smiled, took a few paces back and quietly said, 'Simply unlock the door, Kelly.

Turn the key and open it. You know where we're going. And then put your hands on your head.'

Kelly looked as if he'd sucked on a lemon thinking it was an orange.

He opened the door.

Then Angel directed the man in that pitch-black November evening up the path from the rear of the house to the little car park.

The cold wind was powerful and some of the gusts were wet and salty.

Then Angel said, 'Right, Kelly, take off your coat.'

'Can't do that, Angel. I shall freeze up,' he said.

Angel pointed the gun six inches from Kelly's feet and pulled the trigger. There was a loud report and a few bits of tarmacadam flew up.

Kelly's eyes nearly came out of their sockets. He didn't think that Angel was as severe and ruthless as he proved to be. He'd thought Angel was a pussy cat and was discovering that he was a leopard.

He promptly took off his coat.

'Throw it to me,' Angel said.

He caught it midair.

'Now, turn round and face the wall. Hands back on your head.'

Kelly obeyed.

Using the bonnet of the car as a makeshift table, Angel then went through the pockets of Kelly's coat. He glanced at his wallet. It was stuffed with credit cards and several twenty-pound notes. He put the wallet back. He found Kelly's mobile and put that in his own pocket. He felt justified. It would replace the one Kelly had taken and smashed by stamping on it. There was nothing else of interest.

He returned the coat. Kelly eagerly put it on.

'Now face the wall,' he said, 'and put your hands on your head.'

Angel then opened the car door and from the dashboard pocket he took out a pair of handcuffs and secured Kelly to one of the uprights of the heavy signpost.

'You're not leaving me here like this in this weather, Angel, are you?' Kelly said as he heard him start the car engine.

'Don't worry, Kelly. This is the safest place I could think of. You won't be able to murder anybody from here.'

84

EIGHT

Angel was in position in the car on a lay-by on the coast road a mile from Pilsboro as arranged. He was on the mobile making initial contact with Border Force who look after the UK sea borders. He had already spoken to the duty officer at Scarborough Police.

In his rear mirror, he saw two small, armoured trucks pulled up behind him. He smiled and then sighed. He got out of the car. It was the first time he had felt any relief of any responsibility for the past forty-eight hours. He welcomed DI Waldo White most warmly.

Ten minutes later, Mermaid House was surrounded by armed police and it was not possible for a mouse to escape without White or Angel being aware of it.

Eight powerful spotlights illuminated the rear and front of the house.

A Border Force cutter was a mile out at sea and making fast progress towards Mermaid House.

Angel and White were standing at the back of two small, armoured vans. A sergeant with two armed men were monitoring the rear door of the house. There were more than a dozen armed marksmen from Wakefield and Scarborough forces at specific windows, doors and all other strategic positions.

All the armed men were able to hear and contribute to what was being said among themselves through microphones and earphones.

Angel turned to White and said, 'Did you manage to get a mic in the house?'

'That's the only thing we haven't been able to do. There simply wasn't an opportunity to send a team to safely and covertly find a place on the walls of the building. Nor were there any open windows.'

Then White picked up the megaphone, stepped out from behind the armoured van, put the mouthpiece to his lips and said, 'I am addressing you in Mermaid House. The house is surrounded by armed police. There is no way you can escape. Throw out your guns and come out with your hands on your head.'

A loud shot rang out in the darkness and a wedge of hot lead whizzed through the air. It skidded down the side of the armoured van making a screeching sound. It missed White's head by a few centimetres.

Angel gasped and pulled White to the back of the armoured van and said, 'I thought we had lost you.'

White grinned.

A voice through the headphones called out urgently, 'There's some movement at the back of the house . . .'

It was the sergeant positioned behind rocks at the other side of the house.

Angel and White glanced at each other.

White said, 'Yes? Keep us posted, Peter . . . what's happening?'

'It's the boat, sir. It's edging out from the small entrance to the cave . . . slowly . . . slowly . . . very slowly . . .'

Angel dialled a number on his mobile. It was soon answered. 'This is urgent. Find out the ETA of the Border Force Cutter. I'll hold.'

White adjusted his mouthpiece and said, 'Is it still edging out, Peter?'

'It doesn't seem to be manned,' the sergeant said. 'It's as if it was drifting.'

Angel picked up what was happening and leaned over to White and whispered something in his ear.

White nodded and in the mouthpiece said, 'Is the engine running? Are the propellers moving? Is the water being disturbed at the back end of the boat?'

There was a short pause.

Then the sergeant suddenly said urgently, '*Yes, sir,* I see it now. The water *is* being churned at the blunt end.'

'Right, Peter,' White said.

There was a voice in the earpiece of Angel's mobile. It said, 'The ETA of the Border Force Cutter is six minutes.'

He repeated this to White.

The sergeant monitoring the boat said, 'The boat is in the channel and going towards you.'

Angel said, 'Thank you, Sergeant.'

He turned to White and said, 'So it is being steered. And it is coming briefly towards us. Then there is at least one person aboard the *Marie Celeste*. Can I borrow one of your unit's rifles?'

'Certainly. There's at least one in the back of this van . . . and it will be loaded ready.'

A minute later, Angel was aiming the rifle at the side view of the boat about a hundred and twenty metres away, drifting slowly past.

White said, 'I can't see anybody aboard, Michael. What are you aiming at?'

Angel said, 'Watch the propeller. It has three fins. I hope to shoot them off.'

White grinned. 'You can't even see the propeller. They are under the water.'

'I can.'

Angel stood with his feet apart, the rifle up to his eye. He took aim, squeezed the trigger and watched for the splash in the water. It came but there were still three fins pushing the boat along.

'Missed,' White said.

Angel took another shot.

There was a splash in the water and a very slight ping of contact with metal.

'That's one,' Angel said. 'Watch the boat cruise along more slowly.'

White said nothing.

Angel knew he hadn't time to waste. Another few seconds and he would lose the best angle.

He fired another shot and heard another ping.

White's eyebrows shot up. 'That's two, Michael,' he said.

Angel fired two more shots at the last fin and missed.

However, the speed of the boat had been greatly reduced. If he could hit the third fin the boat could only float with the tide.

He wished the Border Force boat would show itself.

Suddenly, there was the sound of a shot and a lead bullet whistled past Angel's ear.

He was under fire himself by somebody in the house.

He realised that he had taken up a position that enabled him to be a target from the house.

He crouched down to be out of the gunman's range.

Just in time.

Two more bullets passed over his head in rapid succession.

Angel could see that the best opportunity for him to hit that third fin and disable the boat completely was fading rapidly. He must get on with it. It was now or never.

From the crouched position, he could still see the boat. He slowly took aim and squeezed the trigger. He saw the disturbance the bullet had made in the water but there was no sound of it having hit the fin.

White said. 'You might as well give in, Michael.'

Angel's face muscles tightened. 'Not yet.'

The target was very slowly moving away from him and he couldn't actually see the fin on the propeller but he knew it was there.

Angel took careful aim and squeezed the trigger again.

There was no metallic ping.

'Missed. Again,' White said.

Angel took aim and squeezed the trigger again and again and then suddenly there was the elusive ping.

'Bingo!' White said. 'I knew if I goaded you enough you'd do it!'

Angel moved to the relatively safe shelter at the back of the armoured van and put the rifle back in the rack. He wiped his forehead with his handkerchief, then looked down at the boat. It was drifting nowhere. It gave him a warm feeling in his chest. He took out the mobile, dialled a number and said, 'Any update on that Border Force boat?'

'No, sir. But they should be only two or three minutes away.'

'Good. Will you put me through to the captain or officer in charge?'

After a few moments a voice said, 'I am the captain of *Border Force 7*. How can I help you?'

Angel told the captain about the situation and then said, 'Would you seize the boat, arrest whoever is on board — I believe there are two men — and charge them? I must tell you that their land-based partners in crime were heavily armed and very dangerous. They may well be the same. We believe that they have been smuggling drugs from South America. I need to search the boat for drugs or traces of drugs before you tow it away.'

'Certainly,' he said. 'We can do that.'

Angel closed the phone and turned to White. 'What's happening?' he said.

'Nothing,' White said.

'I think there are only two men in the house . . . I only saw two,' Angel said.

Angel thoughtfully reached out for the megaphone. After a few moments, Angel said, 'I'm going to talk to them. It will probably irritate them. In fact, I want it to irritate them, because I want to see where they are. I expect at least one of them will take a pot shot at me in retaliation. Will you carefully watch out for a face, a gun barrel or any movement?'

White pulled a disapproving face. 'I'm not happy at you putting yourself up as a target.'

'Don't worry, Waldo. Watch out.'

'*Don't do it!*' White said.

Angel pulled the megaphone up and pressed the trigger. 'Hello, Foster and Blondie. I know you're in there. We haven't heard from you. If you want to talk about anything, anything at all, shout out that you want to talk and come out unarmed waving something white — a flag or towel — you will be safe. I would be thinking of doing that if I were you.

Have you thought that you cannot escape? There are simply too many armed men here. If you do not surrender voluntarily now, you are very likely to be shot. You may very well have enough provisions for a few days but what's the good of that? You are only delaying the inevitable. How are you going to sleep? Which of you are you going to trust to stay alert? If we made a raid on you, there is no doubt we would overpower you. But we might have casualties and you might have casualties. If you give yourselves up now, you will have to take the punishment for what you have done but you will be certain of living longer. I leave you to think about it.'

Angel switched off the megaphone, waited two seconds then he bobbed down just as a bullet buzzed passed overhead.

White said, 'I saw him, Michael.'

Angel joined White behind the armoured van.

White said, 'I saw the barrel of the rifle poking through the curtains on the corner window on our right on the first floor . . . probably a bedroom. Then, as he withdrew the rifle, he caught the curtain briefly and showed himself to be a small man in a dark suit with a collar and tie.'

Angel nodded. 'That's Foster. He was in charge of this operation. He must be working for Schultz. I am pretty certain that the only other one in the house is a big man called Blondie.'

About ten minutes dragged by, and Angel was thinking about getting some sleep, when White suddenly said, 'Michael, there's something happening. Take a look at the front door.'

The front door was open and a white T-shirt or vest was being waved by a man's big brown arm.

Angel's pulse raced.

White said, 'We might have got a convert.'

Angel quietly said, 'Waldo, order your men to respect the white flag.'

'They know to do that,' White said then he whispered the message, 'Do not shoot, pass it on,' quickly down the line.

Angel reached out for the megaphone. 'You at the front door, we see your white flag. Come out of the house. You are perfectly safe. We will not shoot. Throw out your gun.'

A machine gun rifle and a handgun were thrown from the front door onto the mosaic drive with a clatter.

Angel then said into the megaphone, 'Come on out of the house. You are perfectly safe.'

The man known to Angel as Blondie slowly showed himself in the doorway then came through the door.

'Put your hands on your head and walk to the front gate,' Angel said.

Blondie swallowed hard as he slowly took short steps forward.

White glanced from Blondie to Angel and back and blew out a long sigh of satisfaction as the plan was coming together.

Suddenly, there was the sound of a gunshot.

Angel saw Blondie stop, freeze, his face crease with pain as he collapsed where he stood in the middle of the drive.

White looked round to see who had fired it.

'*Oh no!*' Angel said as he ran his hand through his hair. '*No.*'

Angel's heart pounded. Heat from his heart spread across his chest.

Blondie lay motionless . . . an untidy bundle in the middle of the drive.

White said, 'I know where it came from. The house. The window on our right on the first floor.'

Through gritted teeth Angel said, 'Foster.'

Angel exchanged the megaphone for a pair of binoculars. He looked up at the window and saw a gun barrel showing between the white curtains.

White was on his mobile, calling for an ambulance.

Although he couldn't see Foster, Angel could approximate his position behind the curtain.

Then, unexpectedly, followed a spray of shots from the house in the direction of the armoured vans. Some of the glass in the headlights was smashed and lights extinguished. Everybody ducked out of danger.

White, in a stage whisper, said, 'Anybody hit?'

Two men were hit, but their injuries were small cuts.

Angel breathed in through gritted teeth. Steely eyed, he turned to White and quietly said, 'Waldo, tell your men to eliminate small man in dark suit toting machine gun rifle.'

White whispered the message which was quickly passed down the line.

Angel picked up a rifle from the back of the armoured car, took careful aim at the upstairs bedroom window, and without hesitation, squeezed the trigger. He was accompanied by six other guns . . . some fired a single shot, some went on to give the window a sequence of shots. For a few seconds there was a hell of a racket.

Then it went silent.

The onslaught had caused the window to be greatly damaged. There was very little glass in the frame and very little frame in the brickwork.

Suddenly, a dark-suited arm with a hand at the end flopped out of the hole where the window-frame had been. It was followed by a man's shoulders and a bald head. They hung there limp . . . the arm swinging a little. Drops of blood ran down his arm, through his coat sleeve and across his hand dripping down and splashing on the mosaic drive below.

* * *

Later that day . . .

The inspector from North Yorkshire Police took over the case so far as it involved dealers in drugs and other illegal matters concerning Mermaid House and its recent occupants. He released Kelly, being held captive by handcuffs around the notice board on the small Skye car park. Then he immediately arrested him and charged with dealing in drugs.

DI Waldo White returned with his two ARVs to Wakefield with grateful thanks from Angel. They would be involved in a major investigation into the death of Charles Foster.

The Border Force cutter caught up with the disabled boat and the two crooks, handed them and the boat over to the police, then resumed its usual duties.

Angel was on his way home. After two hours driving, Bridget Dalrymple was still on his mind. How he needed to find her and interview her about the death of Rodney Pertwee. He simply had to bring her in.

Angel was relaxed, already delighted he was so near home, eagerly anticipating holding his wife in his arms and enjoying all the comforts of his home.

He lived in a small bungalow on Park Street on the Forest Hill Estate, Bromersley. The only access road was from a wide opening entrance to the estate from the main Wakefield-to-Barnsley road. He turned the BMW right off the main road, through the entrance to the estate. The road curved round and he came across a big, black car parked up at the side of the road. The man, presumably the driver, was jumping up and down and waving his arms about, begging Angel to stop. He was in his twenties and had a few weeks' beard growth.

As Angel approached the car he saw another man lying in the roadway against the front wheel. He was very still. It didn't look good.

Angel sighed. He stopped the car. The driver rushed up to the car window. Angel opened it.

'Thanks for stopping,' the young man said, pointing at the body on the road. 'I didn't see him coming. He just rushed into the road. He came from nowhere. Never looked to see if any traffic was coming. I've never had an accident before. My licence is absolutely clean. I was only doing about twenty miles an hour. What shall I do?'

Angel saw the curtains of a window of the first bungalow in the estate pulled back and a head and shoulders was looking down on him.

Angel swiftly opened his car door and said, 'Is he dead?'

'Don't know.'

'When did this happen?' Angel said as he rushed across to the man laid out in the road.

'Just now. A minute ago. Two or three minutes ago. No more.'

Angel gently pulled the figure of a man out so that he could see him better.

Then it happened.

The man behind him clenched his fists and, using them as a hammer, came down on the back of Angel's neck. At the same time, the body on the road, which was alive and very well, sprang up and grabbed Angel by the throat.

Angel put his forearms between the second man's hands and slowly pushed them away. While doing so, he noticed that his attacker — the shorter of the two men, who'd previously been the one to play dead — had white paint around the cuticles at the bottom of some of his fingernails. Angel received another thump on the head and neck. It slowed him down for a few seconds. Then he retaliated by pummelling the bearded man hard in the stomach which made him stop.

From the kneeling position, Angel managed to jump up and push the bigger man away, while the painter put up his fists like a fighter and Angel punched him on the nose, which caused him to close his eyes and pull away. The bigger man came forward again and landed a blow on Angel's jaw and made his teeth clatter. Angel gave the man a mighty blow to the stomach. The man doubled up and Angel grabbed him by the waist from behind and half lifted half dragged him onto the grass verge and pushed him into the hawthorn hedge.

In the distance the screech of a police siren could just be heard.

Angel gave a sigh of relief.

As he turned away from the hedge he received a punch in the face from the painter, which smarted. Angel retaliated with a series of blows to the jaw that should have made the man unconscious, but he was still standing.

The man with the beard pulled himself out of the painful thorns on the hawthorn hedge, glared at Angel and crossed the verge to resume the attack.

Angel said, 'What do you want with me?'

The man grinned but he wasn't smiling.

'You gotta to understand that there's plenty more H to come,' he replied and leaped at him.

So heroin was at the root of all this . . . Angel quickly stepped to one side and the man missed him. The man's fist hit the car door handle instead. He nursed his knuckles.

The siren got louder.

Angel then backed him up to the side of the car and pummelled his stomach. Blow after blow in the same spot. The man tried to move out of the way but Angel didn't give him any opportunity.

Then when he least expected it, the man produced a powerful blow to Angel's temple and Angel fell. He blacked out for a moment.

The painter left the scene.

Then Angel saw him.

He was in their car . . . the big black one, in the driver's seat.

'Come on! That's the cops!' he yelled.

The man made for the front nearside door, let himself in and took the seat as the painter started the engine.

Angel recovered from his fall, followed the big man and reached into the car, took hold of his jacket and shirt front with both hands and tried to pull him out. The man gripped hold of the door frame and resisted, then the car began to move.

The siren was much louder. Deafening.

Angel had to walk, then run sideways to keep up with the car. Then he tripped, fell and rolled over to the side of the road into the gutter.

The black car raced away and the door closed.

Moments later, Angel opened his eyes and sat up.

Then a police patrol car stopped just behind him and a uniformed patrolman came quickly up to DI. It was Patrolman Sean Donohue. They were old friends.

'Is it DI Angel? What you doing down there, sir?' he said, assisting him to stand up.

'Did you see a big, black car with two men in it?'

'It was heading up north.'

'See if you can catch and arrest them. They might be armed. Be careful.'

'Right, sir,' Patrolman Donohue said as he rushed back to his police patrol car. 'We will do our best.'

He sped away, his lights flashing and his siren wailing.

NINE

'At last!' his wife, Mary, said as he entered the bungalow.

Angel rushed up to her and kissed her.

'Where *have* you been, darling? You look a mess,' she said.

He looked down at his chest and trousers. Then his hands.

'Just need washing,' he said. 'That's all.'

'Are you sure you are all right?'

'Positive.

'That suit will have to go to the cleaners. I suppose you're hungry?'

'I could eat a horse.'

She put her hands on her hips and said, 'Sorry, sir. Horses are off the menu today . . .'

He feigned disappointment. 'Oh dear . . . '

'I can manage a couple of monkeys or a giraffe,' she said.

He smiled and said, 'No thanks. I had those for breakfast.'

'Get those filthy clothes off. Have a shower and I'll see what I can do.'

'Thank you, sweetheart,' he said and began loosening his tie as he walked out into the hall and through to the bedroom.

* * *

The following morning, Angel was down in his office early. There were several messages waiting for him. There was one from Patrolman Donohue.

It said: 'Sorry, Inspector. I was unable to catch the big black car. I lost them near the junction of the A1 and A66. I spent an hour or so around the junction but could not pick up the trail.'

Angel was disappointed but not surprised.

He then rang Leeds police and was eventually through to the DI dealing with the death of Edward Schultz.

'It looked like an accident at first,' the Leeds DI said, 'but on further investigation it proved to be a possible murder.'

'Did you have any witnesses?' Angel said.

'No. Not exactly. A woman in a green hat carrying a brown paper carrier, with a man in overalls carrying a metal box were seen shortly afterwards leaving the building, but I've no corroboration. Nor have I any idea of their ID.'

Angel's heart began to bang away. Even hearing her description he found himself grinding his teeth. He was angry at his own ineptitude to track Dalrymple down.

'The name of the woman is probably Bridget Dalrymple,' he said, 'but I have no address for her. Nor do I have any info on the man with her.'

'Thank you, Inspector. That's a start.'

Angel replaced the receiver slowly.

He began thinking . . . that woman gets everywhere . . . everywhere where there is murder or evil.

He began wading through his accumulation of post and reading reports when he was interrupted by a phone call from Maurice Mountjoy.

'Ah, Inspector Angel, I was wondering if there was any possibility that I may continue shooting this film I started.'

Angel said, 'We are still making our investigations and all avenues have not yet been investigated. But we will find the murderer, Mr Mountjoy. Don't worry about that.'

'This delay is costing me thousands. All the bills are in for scenery, costumes and there is hire of horses, stabling, feed, to say nothing of the salaries of the cast and crew.'

'We may have to interview more of your people. I'm sorry. I really cannot say.'

'Oh dear. The matter is getting quite desperate, Inspector. You must be able to do something.'

Angel suddenly had a thought. 'Mr Mountjoy, I understand that you know a woman called Bridget Dalrymple.'

Mountjoy sighed. 'I don't *know* her, Inspector. I have met her once in my office.'

'What did she want?'

'She wanted a job.'

'And what did you say to her?'

'All I could say, really. I didn't want to hurt her by saying no, so I said that I would look around. She keeps popping in to see if I have found her anything. It isn't easy to get rid of her. You know, she isn't anybody I would like in my own employment, nor would I like to recommend her to anybody else.'

'If I found her,' Angel said, 'it might enable me to arrest her and tidy up the murders and, of course, you would then be free to continue making the film. I need to find her. Have you got her address?'

'I'm not sure. I think so. Just a minute. It'll be in my address book.'

Angel was excited at the prospect of having Bridget Dalrymple's address. He didn't show it, but he was almost too excited to think straight.

Mountjoy said, 'Yes. I've got it,' he said reading from his address book. It's Dawson Street, Dublin DO2.'

Angel wrote it down, feeling a pang of disappointment that it was Dublin and not the UK.

Then he said, 'Do you not have a local address for her?'

'Sorry,' Mountjoy said.

Angel ended the call.

Then he took out his address book and found the phone number of an Irish policeman, a Garda friend who had been on a case that they had worked on together across the water several years ago. Angel dialled the number which reached the friend straight away.

After reminiscing over old times and past glories, Captain Patrick Devlin said, 'It's a blessing to hear from you, Michael, but what is it that you'll be wanting?'

'And a great pleasure for me to talk to you again, Patrick. What I want is all that you can tell me about a woman called Bridget Dalrymple of Dawson Street, Dublin DO2.'

'From memory, nothing, but that's not far from here. I'll get on to it right away and I'll ring you back.'

As Angel replaced the phone in its holster, there was a knock at the door, it opened and Scrivens put his head in.

'I've got that report on Jimmy Lee, the cinematographer, you wanted, if it's convenient?' Scrivens said, waving a thin beige file at him.

'Come on in, Ted. Of course it's convenient. Sit down.'

He closed the door and sat opposite Angel across the desk.

'Fire away,' Angel said.

Scrivens opened his file and began reading, 'James Lee is forty-eight years of age, brought up in Hong Kong. His father was a diplomat in the British Embassy there. James was educated in the UK. Went to Oxford. Became a Bachelor of Science. Married Judy Wise. Went to Hollywood. Became a gofer, then a microphone holder, and worked his way up to assistant cameraman. Then director of photography. Since then, he's gone from strength to strength and is much in demand. I wouldn't think he's a suspect, sir.'

Angel didn't think it was either, but he just smiled at Scrivens, then nodded and said, 'Even educated people commit murder, Ted.'

Scrivens nodded.

'What do you know about his wife?'

'Judy Wise. A very beautiful woman.'

'What does she do?'

'I don't know that she does anything in particular, sir. She goes with him most places. She is staying with him at Tingle Hall . . . they also have a grown-up daughter. I hear that they are very bored with the situation.'

'Does she mosey along just to spend his money for him?'

Scrivens grinned. 'They've been together a long time. Over twenty years. I don't know what you cynically make of that?'

'I must see them.'

* * *

Next day, as he entered the station, his phone was already ringing. He ran down the corridor, threw open the door and snatched up the phone.

'Angel,' he said.

102

It was Captain Patrick Devlin.

'Regarding Bridget Dalrymple,' he began.

'Ah yes, Patrick.'

'Well, I didn't know, she passed over last year aged sixty . . . a highly respected lady married to a schoolteacher. He passed over three years ago. She supported the church and could often be seen at mass at St Michael's. She taught scripture to the children at Sunday School. It was well known that she enjoyed foreign travel.'

'Anything known?' Angel said.

'Nothing like that, Michael,' the Irish policeman said.

Angel's forehead creased as he considered the information. He was confused.

'Is it possible . . . Could you get me a photograph of her, Patrick?'

'Erm. Oh I could get one from the newspaper. Yes. Or Father Mahoney will know where to find one. Not a problem. Give me a couple of days, Michael. I'll send it over the wire.'

'That's really very good of you, Patrick.'

'Thank you and I owe you one.'

'You're very welcome. Take care now. Goodbye.'

Angel replaced the phone and was overwhelmed by a sudden sense of unease. There was something wrong. He knew he was worried about something . . . something at the back of his mind. Something . . . something intangible. Oh, it wasn't the job . . . it wasn't the woman Dalrymple, that was just work. It was a job. It had its excitements . . . the knowledge that you were serving the decent people in the world and helping to put away those who wouldn't live by the rules. The con men, the thieves, the rogues, the cruel men *and* women, the evil ones. Its opportunities to meet many people . . . but it wasn't worry. Exacting, but not worrying . . . then suddenly it came to him. It was those anonymous letters from Harrogate. And the threat that someone close to him was to kill him. Now that *was* something to worry about.

* * *

Later that day . . .

DI Carter came in. 'You wanted me, sir?' she said.

'Any more news on the Rodney Pertwee murder, Flora?' Angel said.

'Yes, sir. The ballistics report came in. The shot came from a 9mm Glock handgun.'

'Unusual. Anything else?'

'There were no powder marks on Pertwee.'

'Which means the gun man was more than four metres away from the victim.'

Carter nodded.

Angel then said, 'Have you been able to show that Bridget Dalrymple was in the building at that time?'

'Not exactly. We can say that the stage was dark for the night shot, so there were plenty of places, machines, scenery, props, prop baskets and so on behind which somebody with a gun could hide. And there was so much confusion when Pertwee was discovered dead that anyone . . . the gunman or gunwoman . . .could have sneaked out of the stage unnoticed.'

Angel looked down and shook his head. He screwed up his face and said, 'Is that the best you can do?'

DI Carter's muscles round her mouth tightened. 'I can't *invent* evidence,' she said.

'I know you can't, Flora, and I wouldn't want you to. But as it stands it's not going to convince a jury that Bridget Dalrymple murdered him. Have you found a motive?'

Carter's eyes flashed. 'You've only been gone a day,' she said. 'I did all I could.'

'Don't get touchy, Flora,' Angel said. 'I was asking . . .not criticising.'

She settled down. She realised that she might have been hasty.

'It was a busy day,' she said. 'Samantha Rock phoned through to speak to you. They put her on to me, but she specifically wanted you. I told her you were out.'

Angel frowned. 'I wonder what she wanted?'

'Maybe she has some information.'

Angel quickly yanked open a drawer of his desk and took out a telephone directory. 'Originally she booked into the Feathers for the duration of the making of the film, I believe. I wonder if she's still there.'

He found the number and tapped it into the phone. While the number was ringing out, Angel turned back to Carter and said, 'Have you heard anything about the film? Has Mountjoy found a replacement leading man for Pertwee?'

'I think so,' she said. 'Can't remember his name. I've never heard of him.'

'He also needs a director to replace Schultz.'

'I heard that he proposes doing that himself.'

Angel heard the hotel operator speak. 'Sorry, sir. There is no reply from Miss Rock's suite. I should try later.'

'Thank you,' Angel said and replaced the phone.

'Come on, Flora. Let's go to the studio. See what's happening and see if she's there.'

As they went to the door, DS Don Taylor came in with a sheet of paper and a photograph. 'You'll be wanting these, sir. Just arrived addressed to CID.'

Angel took them from him.

The sheet of paper was an email. It was from Captain Patrick Devlin's office, Garda, Dublin. It said, *For the urgent attention of Inspector Angel. Sending pic of Bridget Dalrymple over on email now. Hope it proves helpful. Best wishes, Patrick.*

Angel locked eyes with the woman in the photograph — and felt realisation hit him in an ice-cold wave. His mouth dropped open. She bore no resemblance to the Bridget Dalrymple he'd met here in Bromersley. He reckoned the crook, hearing of the woman's death and respectability, had stolen her identity. He passed the photograph to Flora Carter.

She looked at it, gasped and shook her head.

* * *

Meanwhile, a woman in a green hat, a raincoat and carrying a brown paper carrier bag and a beige paper file got into the lift on the second floor of the Feathers Hotel. There was a man and a woman already there. Seemingly all three were going to the ground floor.

'Good morning,' said Bridget Dalrymple. 'What a lovely sunny day.'

'Good morning,' said the lady. 'It is indeed for November.'

'The Good Lord always looks after us wherever we are, whether we are here or in the beautiful Emerald Isle in these very dark days,' said Bridget Dalrymple.

'Yes. We have a lot to be thankful for.'

The lady adopted a sad face to match the conversation.

Her husband tried not to notice. He stepped back and maintained a steady gaze up to the high corner of the lift.

The doors swished open and the couple made off through the revolving door.

Bridget Dalrymple began quietly humming the hymn *Guide me, O thou great Jehovah*, as she crossed to the reception desk. There was a man in front of her.

As she waited, in her left hand was the ever-present brown paper carrier bag and in the right the file of many A4 sheets of letters and pew sheets. She lifted up her hand, released one side of the beige paper file and allowed the hundred or more letters to flutter to the reception hall floor. There was a bit of a commotion. People from all over the reception area rushed to pick them up and hand them to Bridget Dalrymple who appeared to be embarrassed. Coyly, she thanked each one.

'I don't know what happened. To be sure, you're very kind. Thank you, sir. Thank you, madam.'

The man at the head of the queue to see the receptionist had apparently finished his business with her and went away.

Bridget Dalrymple stepped forward and to the smiling receptionist said, 'I've just seen Miss Samantha Rock. Thank you for your help in that connection. Now, bless you, I have an appointment to see the Bishop and I am late. I don't suppose Saint Peter will wait for me when I am called to the pearly gates. Would it be a trouble to you, dear, to order me a taxi?'

'No trouble at all, Mrs Dalrymple.'

* * *

At ten twenty-five that morning, Angel and Carter arrived at the Northern Film Studios. They were immediately waved through by the uniformed man on the gate.

Angel drove straight to a marked-out parking space outside the sound stage building with the big figure '2' painted on its corner.

As Angel and Carter went into the huge building they could hear a lot of mumbling in one corner of the stage. There was a gathering of the forty cast and crew members standing around in groups of two and three or more talking among themselves.

Angel approached a face he knew and said, 'What's happening?'

It was Ken King, the sound man who positioned a microphone on a pole when filming.

'At half past ten, the boss is going to tell us what his plans are regarding this new film. We expect it will be cancelled . . . that'll put a lot of us looking round for a new job.'

Angel looked at his watch. 'That's in exactly two minutes. Is everybody here?'

'Should be, Inspector Angel. If they value their jobs they should be here.'

'Is Samantha Rock here?'

King frowned. 'I must say I haven't seen *her*. But her agent will probably be told personally by Mr Mountjoy. She'll be on a huge salary . . . I mean, she'll be on a personal contract.'

Carter nudged Angel and said, 'He's here now.'

Maurice Mountjoy came in looking very smart. He looked at the gathering. They all looked at him, looked for the nearest chair and sat down. Somebody pulled out a chair and took it up front for Mountjoy. He put a file of papers on it then turned back to look at the anxious faces.

'Thank you,' Mountjoy said, then he began. 'I am very much wanting to proceed with the making of the film, but as you all know we have lost our leading man, and our director. Now, I have spoken to a possible leading man. He's younger, eager but not anything like as well known as Rodney Pertwee. I won't name him but I can say that he is available and can step in right away if we can agree terms. And I must say, he's very eminently competent. His agent is in touch with me and I am inclined to engage him. Sadly, we have also lost Edward Schultz, a very competent director. If we cannot find a replacement as talented as Mr Schultz in the next few days, I will take on the job of directing in addition to my job as producer.

'Your salaries and wages will be paid up to the end of November. If we are not working . . . normally by then, shall I say? . . . I must give you notice now that I must cancel the film. But I will do everything in my power to proceed with the making and finishing of this film in record time.'

There were a few discontented murmurings among the gathering.

Angel whispered to Carter, 'Can you see Samantha Rock?'

They both looked round at the faces.

Carter shook her head.

Angel whispered, 'Come on. Let's go.'

TEN

Angel and Carter came out of Stage 2 and got into the BMW.

He drove up to the gate and the uniformed man recognised him lifted the bar to allow him to drive out. But Angel stopped halfway through and waved to him to come over.

Angel said, 'You remember me, don't you?'

'You're the detective who is investigating the murder,' he said.

Angel said, 'That woman, Bridget Dalrymple . . .'

'Yes. I remember,' he said. 'She was here a day or so ago. You wanted to catch up with her. I asked her what her business was here. She said she was visiting the HR Department, hopeful of a job in one of the service departments. I asked her where she stayed when she was in Bromersley. She didn't say, but she did say that the Good Lord was sure to provide a bed for her. She talked like that.'

'Huh,' Angel said with a shrug. 'Sounds like she was giving you the brush-off.'

Carter said, 'We still don't know where she lives.'

110

'Perhaps you'll try again, if she returns,' Angel said. 'Tell her it's a requirement of her admission into the studio. My seeing her has become serious. I may have to put out a wanted notice and get the newspapers to publish it.'

The man's eyes opened wide. 'I didn't know it was like that. You surely don't suspect her of murder?'

Angel turned away. He didn't want to answer that. If Bridget Dalrymple heard that he suspected her of murder, she could go to ground and he might never see her again.

Angel looked at the man earnestly and said, 'Do the best you can.' He gave him a business card and added, 'If you see her, give us a call on this number.'

The man took the card and looked at it. 'Will do,' he replied.

'Thanks very much,' Angel said. 'Bye for now.' He engaged first gear and let in the clutch.

* * *

As they reached the police station, Carter made for her desk in the detectives' office while Angel was stopped on the corridor by PC Weightman who said, 'Excuse me, sir. I have just left a note on your desk to say that the super want to see you. I think it's urgent.'

Angel groaned then said, 'Thank you, John.'

Angel pursed his lips in thought then pulled an unhappy face. There was never anything joyful resulting from seeing the super.

He went up the corridor to the super's office. He breathed deeply then knocked on the door and walked into the menthol sanctuary.

The superintendent was working on a pile of papers that almost hid his face.

He looked up. 'Is that Angel? Come in, lad. Where have you been that I can never find you these days. Sit down.'

He picked up the big pile of papers that was masking Angel but couldn't find a place to put it. Angel saw the problem and picked up a much smaller pile thus leaving a space. The superintendent hesitated then took the hint and deposited the big pile there. Angel then handed him the smaller pile. The man took the pile grudgingly not knowing what to do with them. Then he glanced at them to see what they were and eventually found a home for them on top of another smaller pile.

He then sat down carefully positioning his feet to face the blow heater on the office floor.

He said, 'You might like to know that Madigan is still safely boxed up in Durham and has been awarded an extra five years on his term of thirty years. Also I understand that DC Scrivens is fully recovered from his ordeal. If there is nothing else, I can't see why I cannot file this case.'

'There is no reason I can see why you can't, sir.'

'Good,' he said. 'Now, tell me, are you still working on the murder of that film star? What's his name . . .'

'Rodney Pertwee, Sir,' Angel said. 'Oh yes. In fact I think we have enough evidence to make a charge but I am unable to find the suspect.'

'What's his name?'

'It's a woman. Bridget Dalrymple.'

Harker's eyebrows went up. 'Really?' he said. 'Unusual. What's the motive?'

'Don't know, yet.'

'There has to be a motive, Angel. You're not going far without a motive.'

112

Angel impatiently blew out a length of air. 'We're working on it.'

'And what progress are you making on the murder of Edward Schultz?'

'We need to find that woman, Bridget Dalrymple, to progress *that* case. We need to interview her.'

'And what's the motive?'

Angel's lips tightened. 'We're still working on it,' he said.

'Well you *must* have made some progress to justify your expenses partying in Scarborough.'

'There was no partying in Scarborough, sir. I can assure you. We completely cleaned out a big drug distribution cell. And we can now prove that Schultz owned the house where the drugs were stored and sold. I believe he was a big number in the drugs racket here in Yorkshire.'

'I do hope you are watching those expenses,' Harker said.

Angel frowned. He considered replying with something rude, thought better of it and said, 'Oh, I am, sir. Absolutely.'

Harker thought a moment then said, 'I must say, Angel, you're not having your usual good fortune solving these two homicides.'

'We have been most careful with the evidence we have gathered but until we can actually catch Mrs Bridget Dalrymple we are going to continue to be in the dark like this.'

'I am not at all satisfied with your method of investigation.'

Angel wrinkled his nose. 'My method had worked very well indeed in the past. There is not a single case of homicide presented to this department that has not eventually been solved.'

Harker coughed gently then said, 'I believe that's so, but you have two murders here that have stumped you.'

'It's early days, sir. The evidence we have is . . . er, unusual, you could say . . . strange.' Angel then crossed his fingers behind his back and continued, 'But we'll find the murderer and prove the cases eventually. You have my word.'

Before Harker could reply, his phone rang. He reached out for it.

'Yes,' he said. 'What is it? . . . *What!* . . . Rock? . . . Samantha Rock . . . Where? . . . Inspector Angel is with me now. I'll tell him.'

* * *

The following morning, Angel was busy in his office when old Doctor Mac called in. He was carrying a thin beige paper file.

'Hello, Michael. I was just passing. Is it convenient . . . I have finished my post-mortem report on Samantha Rock.'

'Of course,' Angel said. 'You know I am always pleased to see you.'

He pointed to the chair next to his at the desk. 'Sit down.'

The white-haired man put the file he was carrying on the table. He opened it and began. 'It was murder, of course. A perfectly healthy young woman, in an armchair, in her private suite at a highly respectable hotel, choked to death by a big pair of hands. You can see some of the marks still on her throat. I have taken photographs of them.'

Angel pursed his lips and his eyes softened as he imagined the young woman's pain and struggle for breath to survive the attack. Eventually he said, 'You said "big pair of hands", which implies that the murderer was male. Is it not possible then that the murderer was a woman?'

'Perfectly possible,' Mac said. 'There are many women who have big hands.'

Angel was relieved that he would not have to doubt Bridget Dalrymple's probable guilt and have to find another suspect.

'To continue,' Mac said. 'Everything else about the body was remarkably good and healthy. It is a great shame for a young woman to die so young.'

Angel nodded. 'Is there any evidence that suggests Samantha Rock put up a struggle?'

'Not much. There were no signs of bruising anywhere except the throat. Her hands were not bruised nor was there any skin of the assailant under her fingernails.'

Then Mac said, 'Any more questions?'

Angel said, 'Yes. About a million.'

Mac grinned. 'What's the first one?'

'Why does a murderer leave such an obvious trail which always leads directly to her? Most criminals make efforts not to be seen at the scene of the crime, but it seemed that Bridget Dalrymple always wanted it spread far and wide that she was there on the spot with the victim at the critical time. Minutes after this murder, after saying she had visited Samantha Rock, she kicked up no end of a commotion in the hotel foyer.'

'Don't know unless she has a death wish,' Mac said. 'Next question.'

'That's not an answer,' Angel said.

'It's the best I can do. What's your next question?'

'What is the motive for the murder of Rodney Pertwee, Edward Schultz and now Samantha Rock?'

'I don't know. Maybe she's crackers.'

'That's no help at all. For that matter, all murderers are sick in the head.'

'Next question.'

'Why am I receiving letters threatening to kill me? Also I have had a couple of skirmishes with new faces who were also armed.'

'Anybody investigating murder is bound to get in some-body's way. And I have heard you described as the man, like the Mountie, who always gets his man. And you certainly do.'

Angel shook his head and said, 'This is where my run of luck comes to an end.'

The white-haired doctor said, 'Stick with it, Michael. There'll be a reason for all these unusual circumstances. I'm sure that you will find out in the end.'

* * *

Dr Mac returned to the mortuary and Angel was able to get to the day's post.

As he quickly cast his eyes through the small pile of letters and packets, he saw another envelope personally addressed to him in that same unusual script and postmarked Harrogate which caused his heartbeat to race. He picked out the envelope and dropped it on the desk. He stared at it for a few moments. He wanted to call out but he didn't know what to say or who would hear him. He rapidly opened the middle desk drawer and took out a letter opener. He quickly poked it into the cor-ner of the envelope and slid it across. He took out the single sheet of paper. It was written by hand in block letters.

It said:

I HAVEN'T FORGOTTEN YOU, ANGEL. THERE HAVE ALWAYS BEEN WITNESSES AROUND. I WILL KILL YOU AT THE NEXT OPPORTUNITY . . . WHEN WE ARE ALONE.

Same as the others, it was unsigned.
Angel's face muscles tightened.

116

He closed his eyes and began to go through all the people he had seen in the past week . . . particularly in situations where he was with one person at a time. There were a dozen or more encounters he could recall. They all seemed friendly. The exercise didn't point up the killer.

He gritted his teeth, then ran his hand through his hair. He pushed the letter roughly back in the envelope, shoved it into the drawer with the other two and slammed the drawer shut.

He tried to pretend that that was the end of it, but he knew it wasn't. The letters were clearly from a nutcase. He was thinking. What murderer goes around telling the victim in advance that he was going to kill him? The murderer would surely want the element of surprise to be an advantage? Even so . . . an experienced, highly confident man . . . or woman . . . perhaps he or she didn't think they needed that advantage.

There was a knock on the door and Carter breezed in. She was waving several sheets of A4 paper around. 'I've got something that you might find interesting, sir.'

Angel looked up at her. He was thinking. He didn't want to look at something *interesting* . . . he could do with some reliable information that would lead to the location of Bridget Dalrymple.

'What is it, Flora?'

'That cinematographer, James Lee, with that film company?'

'Yes, go on, Flora.'

'Well, sir. Seems that after his years at university he began a publishing business. He published a magazine strangely called *No Staples*. It was really a massive poster that folded down rather like an old road map to look like a book. When opened right up, each side had a large picture of a nude girl.'

Angel wrinkled his nose. 'I expect it sold like hot cakes.'

'Apparently, the first edition did, but the second and third editions finished up on a massive bonfire. Mothers, grandmothers, wives and girlfriends did not approve of the massive photograph on their bedroom walls.'

Angel agreed with the womenfolk. 'Another win for your gender.'

Carter smiled coyly. 'Of course,' she said then she added, 'But there is more, sir. Shortly after that, James Lee was arrested and charged with possession of Class C drugs. However, the case was not proved. He was found not guilty and discharged. He immediately left for Hollywood.'

'I bet it was as fast as his little boots would take him,' Angel said.

'Not quite. He married Judy Wise. Comes from an old English family. She gave him a measure of respectability.'

'And a fat portfolio of property, shares and money, I guess,' Angel said.

Carter smiled and said, 'Why are you always so cynical?'

Angel looked up and said, 'Why? Am I right?'

'Annoyingly,' she said, 'you are *not* wrong. How do you do it, sir?'

'Guesswork, I expect. What else?'

'Educated at a convent school, went to Switzerland for polishing, then Oxford, married at twenty.'

'Does she dirty her hands with work?'

'Tut-tut, sir,' she said, 'do I also detect sarcasm?'

'Well, *does* she?'

'Not now,' she replied with a grin. 'She did. She worked for a charity.'

'And gave it up to get married!' he said boldly.

'And now fortune telling,' she said. 'I didn't know you could tell fortunes, sir. Yes, that's right. Also she is an amateur watercolour painter and is building something of a reputation. I hear she's no Picasso but does some interesting work.'

Angel's eyebrows shot up. 'Really? Most interesting. I must invite her to meet my wife who dabbles in watercolour painting.'

* * *

A church clock in the distance chimed. It was five o'clock. The end of another dark, working November day. Angel looked up from the report he was reading, put a used, empty envelope between the pages to mark how far he had read, cleared his desk then reached out for his hat and coat from the peg on the side of the stationery cupboard, switched off the light and closed the door. He went up the corridor, past the cells to the rear entrance. He flashed his card at the automatic lock, it clicked, the door opened revealing the black, starry sky. He made his way out into the cold.

An outside lamp illuminated the police station private car park and pound. The park was about half full. Angel's car had an allotted space which was about thirty metres from the rear entrance.

He made his way across it when he heard a gunshot close by and felt a slight rush of air as a bullet passed his left ear lobe and deposited itself noisily two metres away in the station wall.

Angel dropped to the ground and crawled round the back of his car in time to avoid a second bullet which landed about a centimetre from the first.

His heart beat as fast as a racing helicopter.

That second bullet indicated the approximate position of the gunman. He worked out that the gunman was at the pedestrian entrance to the police park. Angel saw a shadow of him peering round the entrance. He wished he had a handgun to be able to retaliate.

He took out his smart phone and dialled DS Carter.

'Flora,' he whispered. 'Somebody with a gun has got me pinned down outside on the car park, behind my car.'

'Some of us thought we heard shots,' she said.

'Don't let anyone leave the station and walk into him. Quickly withdraw a rifle from armoury and carefully try to move him on. He *was* at the entrance to the car park at the front. Be very careful.'

'Take a couple of minutes,' Carter said.

Angel breathed deeply and wondered who it could be that wanted him dead.

He shuffled silently on his hands and knees in and among the parked cars.

He thought he heard a footstep quite close. His heart raced as he held his breath, listened and waited.

He couldn't hear anything but the drone of distant traffic in the town.

From a squatting position he put his head up a few centimetres looking for the person with the gun. There was nobody there. He became bolder. He stood up, looked round and listened.

A short distance away, he heard a voice with an Irish accent say, 'I've got to get out of here — and fast! The man has vanished into thin air. Would you believe it?'

Angel blinked, then out loud said, *'Bridget Dalrymple.'*

He wanted her.

Then he saw the silhouette of Flora Carter with the Heckler and Koch rifle. She was holding it in at her waist . . . a good firing stance . . . making her way along the path into the car park, he thought.

From the street at the front of the station, a car door slammed, an engine revved and with squealing tyres the car sped away.

Angel ran to the park entrance and saw the back of an old, big, black car with a square licence plate.

He turned back and made for his own BMW, calling, 'Flora! Quick. Come with me.'

They both got into the BMW. Then Angel raced the car out of the police park.

The streets were dark and there was a lot of traffic to overtake. It was the busy hour. Very soon, the back of the big, old car came into his view. He sighed with relief and began to breathe evenly. He hoped that Bridget Dalrymple hadn't seen them. Keeping an eagle eye on the black car, he dropped back to allow a large van to cover between them. He followed the car through the town centre to York Road where the traffic began to thin out. Following covertly became more difficult. After twenty minutes or so, Angel realised he had been spotted when the big car increased its speed and was driven erratically . . . jerking to the left and then to the right. Angel's BMW was able to keep up with most any car on the road. So Bridget Dalrymple soon gave up that strategy to escape.

Between stretches of houses, they were passing factories, warehouses and small areas of green field. Suddenly, the big car slowed down and turned into the short drive and big gate to the Northern Film Studios. The gate poles were up in the air to admit easy admittance of cleaners, rubbish collectors and delivery of difficult loads.

Angel started to turn the wheel to follow.

Carter looked at him and said, 'Do you think this is a trick?'

'I don't know, but what else would I do?' Angel said. 'I've got to arrest that woman.'

Bridget Dalrymple drove the big car to the far end of the site and then turned left then again at the following corner.

Angel slowly drove only a short way and slowed the BMW at each corner the big car took.

A shower of hot lead came almost before he had pulled on the brake. He reversed behind the sound stage building.

'Down!' Angel shouted at Flora Carter. She made herself as small as possible in the seat well.

The Heckler and Koch repeater rifle was on the back seat. Angel reached out for it and leaped out of the car. From behind the open car door, he fired a retaliatory spray of bullets in the direction of the driver's window of the big car not knowing if the driver was there or not. The rifle had superb night lenses but there simply wasn't sufficient light to see much detail through them at that distance.

Then all was quiet.

Carter, keeping low, got out of the car and came up beside Angel.

'What's happening?' she asked.

'I don't know,' Angel said as he peered down the rifle sight. Then Angel saw the movement of a figure between the big car and the building. He let off another short spray of bullets.

Then everything was very quiet again.

Angel did not know whether Dalrymple was still with the car or had entered the sound stage.

He would have to watch his ammunition . . . he didn't know how many bullets were in the rifle cartridge.

He suddenly saw a flash of light inside the sound stage. 'She must have entered the building,' he said. Then he added, 'Flora, you stay here. I will have to follow her into this place. Can't think why she came here. I don't know what to expect.'

'You can expect a bullet in your back, sir, if you're not careful.'

Angel grinned then said, 'Always so cheerful!'

Holding the rifle at his waist, Angel went up to the door of the sound stage. It was wide open, the cleaners letting some fresh air get into the place. He peered around the black outlines of cameras, recording equipment, still photo cameras, scenery and props looking eerie in the dark.

He looked and listened for a while. He heard nothing.

At the far side of the building was the light. It looked as if it was from an office.

As he approached the office he heard from outside the unmistakable roar of the big black car being started, followed by the low hum and the regular click of tappets as it passed the open entrance behind him.

Angel gritted his teeth. His fists tightened. In the darkness Bridget Dalrymple had got away. He couldn't possibly race back to his car and catch up with her now. He thought a few moments and decided to continue investigating the light in the office.

Then suddenly he heard a small movement among the sheets covering some studio equipment. It was about four metres behind him. He gripped the rifle tight and froze.

It wasn't repeated. Everywhere was still and quiet.

Angel allowed several more seconds to elapse before taking a few more steps forward towards the light.

As he moved, a dust sheet over one of the machines behind him slithered to the floor. He turned and saw it finish its fall.

Angel reckoned he wouldn't be fooled a third time . . . there was definitely somebody there. He raised the rifle.

'I have a rifle pointed directly at you,' he said. 'Come out or I will squeeze the trigger.'

'Oh sir, it's me,' Carter said her face going red. 'I didn't mean to . . .'

Angel sighed. 'Oh Flora,' he said, shaking his head and lowering the rifle.

She said, 'I came in to tell you that the big car has gone.'

ELEVEN

It was 10 o'clock on Friday morning . . .

The phone rang. Angel reached out for it.

It was a young PC on reception. 'There's a gentleman here who wants to see you, sir. Says his name is Maurice Mountjoy.'

'Bring him down to my office, Constable, please.'

Angel turned to Carter and said, 'It's Mountjoy in reception.'

'I wonder what he wants?'

'He might have some information.'

Maurice Mountjoy looked as smart as a new pin but with a very worried look betrayed by the creasing of the eyes. He came straight to the point.

'I need your help, Inspector. I hope you will realise . . . I suppose you have *already* realised . . . the troubles I have trying to progress the production of my new film. Both my leading stars and an important member of the crew have been most cruelly murdered. I have to replace them, which isn't easy. Also costs go on . . . the hire of the studio, the salaries of the entire staff continue. This is extremely expensive. It is a great worry. I have to ask, how much longer is this going on?'

'I wish I knew, Mr Mountjoy,' Angel said. 'My team and I are working full time on this case and we hope to make an arrest soon.'

Mountjoy's face brightened. 'You mean you have a suspect?'

Angel tried to avoid answering supplementary questions. The sparseness of the reply invariably encouraged the questioner to make assumptions that were incorrect.

'We hope to make an arrest soon,' he repeated.

'I know that the police are a charitably minded organisation . . . I would be happy to make a substantial donation to your favourite charity if you could wind this case up in the next week.'

Angel smiled. 'That would be most welcome,' he said. 'It would be difficult to specify a date, but, as I said, we hope to make an arrest soon.'

* * *

It was Sunday evening and Bridget Dalrymple was among the tiny congregation who attended the service at St Patrick's Church in Bromersley town centre.

So was the cinematographer, James Lee. He was unaccompanied and seated ten rows in front of Bridget Dalrymple. She had her eyes on him throughout the service.

The priest announced the last hymn, *The Day Thou Gavest, Lord, is Ended,* which the small congregation sang weakly, then sat down. The priest then delivered the final prayers and a blessing.

The service was over.

The small congregation finished their own prayers and began to leave their pews, deliver their books to the verger at the back of the church and then make for the door.

Bridget Dalrymple put her own prayer book into her big brown paper carrier then took out a large, freshly laundered gentleman's handkerchief from her handbag. She discreetly opened the handkerchief to reveal a handgun. She held the gun covered by the handkerchief, closed her handbag and hung it on her arm.

The organist played the *Alleluia Chorus* very loudly to accompany the leaving of the congregation.

She checked the whereabouts of Mr Lee.

He was still in his pew.

The priest was now at the door, and a small queue had formed to speak to him.

Lee left his pew and made for the door.

She quickly left her pew but in her bid to reach Mr Lee, she forgot a small brown paper bag alongside where she had been sitting. She rushed down the aisle, timing it so that she was immediately behind Lee in the queue to speak to the priest.

As she stood in the draughty doorway behind Mr Lee and looked outside, she saw a black sky with many sparkling stars. At the same time, the organ was blaring out the music, louder than ever.

Mr Lee had reached the priest and after reciprocal exchanges, Lee took his leave and made his way through the old porch into the night.

It was at that point that Bridget Dalrymple raised her hand holding the gun. She pointed it at James Lee and squeezed the trigger.

A loud report echoed round the vaulted porch.

Lee cried out. He fell down face first on the stone porch floor.

Bridget Dalrymple ran through the porch out into the night.

The priest quickly kneeled down to assist Lee.

He turned him over in his lap.

Lee's linen shirt was a bright red.

There was nothing the priest could do but pray.

Outside, at the side of the road was a big car which had a door open and a driver with the car engine running. Bridget Dalrymple climbed in and was away in seconds.

* * *

Angel was notified of the murder minutes after it had happened and began the usual procedures without much enthusiasm until the verger came up to him.

'Are you the Inspector dealing with this murder?' he said.

'I am,' Angel said.

From under his long black verger's robe he pulled out a crumpled brown paper bag. 'From that seat where that murderer sat I found this bag. In her hurry, she forgot to take it with her.'

He handed the paper bag to Angel.

Angel peered into the bag. It contained an unopened cellophane packet of ladies' silk stockings.

The following morning, the national newspapers were full of the news of another murder, and so were the locals, television news and radio.

Angel had several eyewitnesses and took their statements. He also notified Doctor Mac, the pathologist and went through the routine with him.

He told Carter about the stockings and showed her the packet.

He said, 'I want you to get all the personnel you can muster and see if you can find out the shop or store who stocked this brand of stockings. I should like to speak to the salesperson who actually sold them to Bridget Dalrymple yesterday, Sunday. I assume she bought them on Sunday. Of course she could have bought them earlier but why would she walk around with them and take them to church with her?'

* * *

It didn't take long for the police to find out who sold the stockings. It was the owner of a tiny haberdashery in an arcade that also stocked bow ties, cravats, braces, club ties, cuff links, tie pins, suspenders and stockings and so on.

Angel and Carter didn't waste any time getting there and reading the sign over the shop window. *STRENG & SON, SPECIALIST HABERDASHERS. EST. 1906.*

They went into the shop and looked around. It was tiny but very tidy, clean, and the shelves were simply bursting with stock. They went up to the counter which was a glass showcase. At that moment, the shop had no customers. A small man about sixty years of age came forward.

'Good afternoon, sir — and madam. I am Ernest Streng, proprietor. Can I help you?'

Angel held up his warrant card and flashed it at the man. 'We are police officers, Mr Streng. I understand that yesterday you sold these silk stockings to a woman in a green hat?'

Carter held out the packet for Mr Streng to take.

The small man took the packet. He looked at the front then turned it over and looked at the back.

'Ah yes,' he said. 'One of your detectives told me that his boss would be calling on me. I believe I sold these stockings to an Irish lady yesterday afternoon. Is there anything wrong, Inspector?'

'Not at all, Mr Streng. The transaction and the stockings appear to be perfectly all right . . . we are interested in the *woman*. What can you tell me about her?'

Streng frowned and pursed his lips. 'She was just a very talkative Irish woman.'

'Did she say anything about her life or lifestyle? Did she say where she lived? Did she indicate where she was staying?'

'No, but she *did* say that she was going to Saint Mary's later and needed to look appropriately smart to be "present before the Lord". She talked like that.'

Angel's face hardened. 'That's the one we are after.'

Carter made a note on her clipboard.

'Did she say anything else?' she said.

'She said lots of things, Inspector. Mostly inconsequential chit chat.'

Carter said, 'We are interested in tracing her whereabouts, Mr Streng. Did she do or say anything to you that would help us to find her?'

'It seems very important to you,' Streng said.

Angel said, 'Oh, it is.'

Streng's mouth opened. His eyes shone. He looked at Carter then at Angel and said, 'Well, I remember she said something about a wife. I think she said that somebody's wife turned round and was instantly turned into a pillar of salt. I didn't know quite what she was talking about.'

Carter and Angel exchanged glances. This wasn't helping them.

'And she talked about two sisters, Mary and Martha,' Streng said. 'One was always on her knees praying while the other one was doing all the household chores. Somebody was making a comparison of some sort.'

Angel said, 'Yes, but did you see or hear anything that might assist us to reach her now?'

'No. But there was something else. There was one thing.'

Angel looked up. 'What was that?'

'When she came to pay for the stockings, I noticed that she was wearing an excessive amount of make-up.'

Angel sighed. 'A lot of make-up?'

'Yes. I reckon you could have scraped it off her face with a knife.'

'If she returns, please give us a call,' Angel said, placing a business card on the counter.

Angel and Carter took their leave of Mr Streng and returned to the car parked at the bottom of the of the arcade in town. Angel drove the car back to the station.

He was met by an anxious DC Scrivens. 'Thank goodness you're back, sir,' he said. 'The super wants to see you, urgently.'

Angel frowned. He wondered what he wanted this time. He wasn't pleased. Superintendent Horace Harker rarely wanted to see him about anything that progressed the investigation of a case he was working on.

He immediately went along the corridor up to the super's office, knocked at the door and went in. The super's desk was its usual mess, the menthol smell as pungent and the hum of the two blow heaters irritating.

Harker was working at his desk. He glanced up at Angel and said, 'Sit down.'

'You wanted to see me, sir?' Angel said.

'How far are you on with that case? I am getting a lot of pressure from London.'

'We know the identity of the murderer, sir.'

'A woman, amazingly,' Harker said. 'I have read your report.'

'We've got eyewitnesses . . .exceptional witnesses . . . different for each of the four murders. But we cannot find the woman.'

'What's the motive?'

Angel shuffled uneasily in the chair. 'We haven't that either.'

Harker threw down his pen. 'The job's only half done, Angel. The victims were all vital contributors to that new film that Maurice Mountjoy is trying to make aren't they? Isn't there a motive in there somewhere?'

'No sir. Every obstacle put in Mountjoy's way risks the cast and crew their jobs, and, although they are very well paid when working, they have to fight for work when unemployed . . . which is most of the time. The strange thing is . . . this woman always kills the victim deliberately . . . in public, in front of an audience, you might say. Whereas every other murder I have ever been working on the murderer has tried to conceal his or her guilt. She parades it.'

'What am I to tell the Chief and the Commissioner?' Harker said.

'The truth, sir. It would be helpful if he gave us more men so that we could start a door-to-door.'

'He won't do *that*. The government and the Met have got their own money troubles.'

'Well,' Angel said, 'I think that now we should appeal to the public via the press.'

'Very well, do that. But for goodness' sake, get the case solved, charge the woman and let's get on with things.'

'I will do, sir, *when* we get the evidence.'

'Now leave me. Let *me* get on,' Harker said. 'I have work up to my eyes. I have a much bigger problem than you have.

I have to find a conjuror for the children's Christmas party.
They are all booked up!'

Angel came out of the office grinding his teeth. He
stormed down to his office noisily closing the door.

* * *

At 10.30 that evening, after supper, Angel and Mary went
into the sitting room. Angel picked up the local newspaper
and glanced at the front page. Mary snuggled up next to him
on the sofa, switched on the television and tapped the remote
several times trying to find a programme of interest. After
few tries she finished up with a repeat of repeats, a film with
Randolph Scott. She was soon snoozing. After twenty minutes
or so, disturbed by a loud advertisement on the TV she woke
up. She suddenly opened her eyes, looked at Angel and said,
'I'm going to bed, sweetheart. I'm absolutely bushed.'

Angel was pleased he was married to Mary. She was very
understanding.

'Yes, love,' he said. 'So am I. Right behind you.'

Minutes later they were undressed and in bed. He turned
out the bedside light. Mary was on her side, eyes closed and
falling rapidly to sleep. Angel was on his back, gazing in the
direction of the ceiling, thoughts of Bridget Dalrymple still
chasing through his head.

A few hundred sheep later, he was still awake. How on
earth was he going to catch her? Her very *identity* was a lie. He
had never had a situation where the villain seemingly wanted the
police to have eyewitnesses to their murders. That's what Bridget
Dalrymple seemed to have arranged for each murder. Why? And
what motive could be behind her crimes? Each murder slowed
down or stopped the making of a film. Bridget Dalrymple was a

thorn in the side of the producer, Maurice Mountjoy. That man had to find a replacement every time there was a murder. The delay will up the production costs considerably.

If Bridget Dalrymple wanted rid of Maurice Mountjoy, she could have made him the victim instead of four of the talented, key personnel. And something told Angel she wasn't finished there. Nothing logical fit any explanation that Angel could come up with. And why couldn't he find her? All the police at the station had been notified, as had the National Crime Agency. But they hadn't a photograph of her — the image of the *real* Bridget Dalrymple he'd had from Ireland was no use to him, of course — nor had she been seen since the murder of Samantha Rock. The situation was difficult.

Also he was thinking about the constant threat on his own life.

The fact that the envelopes of the three notes vowing to kill him were stamped with a Harrogate postmark wasn't necessarily a clue. A man living in Bromersley could make the trip to maintain the secrecy. Angel never knew when or where he was being watched. There were times . . . particularly in the dark . . . he felt acutely vulnerable.

He closed his eyes.

He swallowed. His mouth felt like a lime pit so he made a decision. He was going to make a cup of tea.

He gently unravelled himself from Mary, sat up, turned and sat on the edge of the bed in the dark.

He suddenly felt some movement of the duvet behind him. A sleepy voice said, 'If you're making some tea, darling, bring me a cup.'

It was Mary.

Angel smiled then he said, 'I thought you were in the land of Nod.'

He switched on his bedside lamp.

'I was,' Mary said, screwing up her eyes, 'until a herd of elephants started bouncing around on the bed. Anyway, why can't you sleep?'

'It's this case, love. I'll get the tea.'

Five minutes later he brought a tray in with two mugs of tea.

After Mary had heard all about Angel's problems finding Bridget Dalrymple and her guilt in the murder of Rodney Pertwee, Edward Schultz, Samantha Rock and James Lee, she said, 'Maybe this Bridget Dalrymple doesn't exist.'

Angel's eyes opened even further. He banged the mug down on the tray.

'I've seen her,' he puzzled. 'We've spoken to each other. She's attacked me! I have signed statements from witnesses who say that they have seen her. Somebody has almost always been present when she actually commits the murder.'

Mary said, 'I don't doubt that. I am not doubting anything you have said, dear. Even so, she still sounds ethereal, insubstantial . . . I can't think of the word . . . false. And you never said she had attacked you.'

Angel pulled an unhappy face. 'You wouldn't say that if you had seen her. I reckon she's as hard as the Rock of Gibraltar, and a murderer to boot.'

Mary said, 'All that appearing here and there . . . bobbing up and down . . . but never in a situation where you can slip on the handcuffs.'

They were both silent and thoughtful for a while and sipped the tea.

Angel was also considering how the threatening letters to him bearing a Harrogate postmark fitted into this case, and whether he should tell Mary about them. He quickly decided against it. She was upset enough with him being a detective with the police as it was. She always considered it a highly dangerous job.

Mary was thinking that from her husband's detailed description of Bridget Dalrymple there was something extraordinary, unusual about her . . . but she couldn't put it into words.

Eventually she said, 'I think what I am trying to say is that I should look for another motive. I think that that would help you to sort this case out.'

Angel shook his head. 'I don't know what you mean, love. This case is about sewn up if I can arrest the woman and charge her. But I simply can't find her. Nobody seems to know where she is staying or anything about her whereabouts.'

Mary stifled a yawn, but Angel saw it.

'Leave it with me,' he said.

He kissed her on her forehead.

They both settled down. Angel switched off the light.

'Goodnight, darling,' she said. 'I hope you have a good night.'

They both nodded off to sleep.

* * *

First thing next morning, Angel quickly assembled raincoat, carrier bag, hat and wig, and enrolled a female colleague, thought to be close to Bridget Dalrymple's size, to wear them. He put a plain sheet of white paper across the woman constable's actual face like a mask and had the police photographer make twenty prints of the woman.

Then he phoned the three local papers and asked them to help. He gave their reporters all the relevant facts about the murders, explained about the photograph and they all said they would use it. He sent a copy of everything by email and he gave his personal telephone number as the contact number.

The appeal for the whereabouts of Bridget Dalrymple, with the photograph, came out in the three newspapers the following day, and when Angel saw the reports he was quite excited.

There were only three phone calls in response to the appeal. Two of them wanted to know if there was a reward — which there wasn't — so their calls ended without offering any information.

The third immediately said that she had seen a woman answering the description.

She said, 'I have seen her several times entering the old Albury House buildings. She was usually in a big, black limousine.'

Angel grinned. 'At last!' he said loudly.

TWELVE

The Albury House buildings was an estate of forty flats on the fringe of Bromersley built by the council in 1945. It was tacked onto a small estate of terraced houses. It was built with the good intention of providing accommodation for the returning troops who had lost their homes due to the war. However, they were badly planned and badly built. For one thing, there was nowhere to park a car. Another, no grass or park nearby for children to have a game, a kickabout or any other similar pleasure. And there was no central heating. Consequently, it was not the most popular accommodation.

The buildings were surrounded by NO ENTRY signs and netted wire fencing which over the years had in places had been pulled down, flattened and driven over.

Angel was eager to search the block, but that could be a very dangerous operation as there were simply too many damaged windows and doors to provide shelter in any gun play. In addition, there were too many passages leading everywhere and an abundance of illicit entrances and exits. He would need a platoon of men to search the place safely. He would give it a lot of thought.

* * *

The following night . . .

Bennie Jones opened the kitchen door at the rear of the Feathers Hotel and went outside into the night. He leaned against the wall of the hotel, looked up at the spread of bright stars on the black sky and in a loud voice said, 'Come out here, Aaron. Nobody can hear us. I want a word.'

Aaron Penn came out of the back door of the Feathers Hotel and stopped by the rubbish bins against the wall.

'What do you want?' he said.

Old Norman was only three metres away. He was sitting on a flattened Weetabix cardboard box, his back against the hotel wall. He silently rolled to one side, pressed himself behind two rubbish bins and remained motionless.

'It's time we got rid of Angel,' Jones said.

Norman was shocked at what he heard. He recognised the unmistakable, high-pitched voice of Bennie Jones. He had heard him before, but he didn't know the man.

'He's getting too close for my liking. All these near misses,' Jones continued, 'might just result in a bit of bad luck next time and things could go wrong. If that happens we'll be right in it.'

Penn said, 'Well, I'll watch my bloody step, Bennie. I'm not going back inside for anybody. I'll get my share of the take and then I'm off. You won't see me for dust.'

'Roll on the day,' Bennie Jones said. 'What about Angel?'

'Are you serious? Are you talking about rubbing out that copper? That's thirty years if we're caught, you know.'

'I feel he's getting too near, don't you?'

'Have you a plan?'

'Sort of . . . Well, you know he's as mad as crazy to want to catch our Bridget?' he said with a grin.

Aaron Penn nodded. 'Go on,' he said.

'Well, if we plant info . . . *false* info for Angel to hear, that our Bridget will be at a certain place at a certain time . . .'

'It's been done before,' Penn said.

'This is different.'

Aaron Penn listened carefully to Bennie Jones's plan.

Old Norman strained to hear every detail. He waited while they retired and all in the yard was quiet then he pushed away the cardboard cover, phoned the police station and eventually was able to pass the details of what he had heard to Angel.

* * *

The following morning, Angel arrived at the office, parked the car in his usual allotted parking space close to the police building in the car park. He went straight into the station through the rear door which had a security porthole fitted. He opened it as soon as he had closed the door and peered out at the many police vehicles as well as civilian cars already parked up there.

He didn't seem to see anything of interest.

The nearest pub to Bromersley Police Station was the Bull.

At lunchtime that's where you would usually find Angel. And that day was no exception.

Opting to use the rear door of the station, Angel took the opportunity to look over the police vehicle car park. He paid particular attention to his own car. But there wasn't anything amiss.

At about six o'clock, Angel finished reading the PCs' reports. He closed them up and put them in a drawer. He put on his overcoat, gloves and hat, and made for the rear door of the Station.

That November evening the sky was as black as an undertaker's hat.

Angel switched on the powerful lights that swept across the police car park. Everything seemed quiet. There were still lots of cars parked there but no signs of life. He switched off the lights, stepped outside and closed the door. He heard the crack of a gun in the distance, the sound and passage of a shell as it sped past his right ear and the solid thud of the bullet embedding itself in the door jamb.

He promptly dropped to the floor and scrambled on hands and knees amidst the parked cars. His heart thumped away. His breathing was erratic. His face, neck and ears felt impossibly hot. He was surprised but not injured. He wondered who the shooter was.

Unsurprisingly, there were four more gunshots in quick succession aimed around the rear entrance of the police station.

On his hands and knees in the dark, on the ground, through the many parked cars, he kept on the move, taking an erratic path towards the far end of the park. At one point he carefully peered up above a car bonnet and saw the silhouette against the window light. He instantly recognised it as that of the big man, Bennie Jones. He was over six feet tall and probably weighed over eighteen stone.

Angel was almost at the back boundary wall of the car park. He remained motionless and listened for a minute or so. All he heard was the drone of traffic from the town centre. He had no weapon. Nothing to compare with a loaded handgun. Then he moved quickly away, dodging behind the front wheels of a car and then he rested. After a few seconds he heard the rustling of Jones's clothes. And shortly after that, his laboured breathing.

He moved on and when he was only four cars away, Angel sensed that he was working his way into a corner. He stopped to consider his next move. He heard the heavy breathing of Bennie Jones advancing towards him.

His own heartbeat was stronger and faster.

Then suddenly, through the gap in a car wheel, he saw the round face of Bennie Jones.

But the big man had seen him first.

He pointed the gun at Angel and squawked, 'Don't try anything clever. Put your hands where I can see them.'

Angel had no option.

'Now stand up,' Jones said. 'Slowly . . . very slowly.'

They stood up together. They were facing each other.

Bennie sniggered and said, 'Well, well, well. I've got the famous Inspector Angel at the end of a gun. They'll never believe it.'

Suddenly, the powerful car park lights went on the and through a loudspeaker the voice of Detective Sergeant Flora Carter was heard to say, 'But not for long, Mr Jones. Drop the gun.'

Bennie Jones sucked in a quick breath. He looked round to find Carter, Scrivens and Taylor positioned at three of the corners of the car park each holding a loaded assault rifles at the waist, all pointed at him.

His eyebrows shot up.

'Don't shoot!' he screamed. 'For God's sake, don't shoot.'

He dropped the gun and put up his hands.

* * *

142

It was ten o'clock that evening before Angel had finished the paperwork and the cross examining of Bennie Jones. However, he didn't find out anything he didn't already know. He charged Jones with murder and four other minor related charges. And he arranged for him in to appear on the Magistrates' Court list the next day.

He was about to leave the cell in Bromersley Police Station when Jones said something unusual. 'Angel, if I tell you summat that will possibly save one of your copper's lives . . . would it do me any good? Would it shorten my time in the pokey?'

Angel said, 'If it was really a genuine, provable saving, it most certainly would. The judge would be advised and it could make a significant difference to your sentence.'

Jones wrinkled his nose, pursed his lips and rubbed his chin. Then he said, 'I must say my solicitor is dead against me trying to do a deal. I will have to trust you.'

Angel looked at him and said, 'You can do that . . . but only if you're genuine.'

Bennie nodded. He seemed satisfied.

'That sergeant you have . . . Carter,' he said. 'She comes to work in a car. She keeps her car outside on a patio space.'

Angel's heartbeat increased.

'Go on,' Angel said.

Bennie Jones looked at the clock on the wall.

'By now the car will have a bomb placed under the driver's seat. It will explode when she switches on the ignition. She should use the bus for once in the morning.'

Angel immediately rang Carter at home. 'Bennie Jones has just told me that there is a bomb under the driver's seat of your car. So don't go near it. I shall immediately advise the bomb disposal people. They'll come out straight away. If it's not been made safe by early tomorrow morning, you'd better come in by bus.'

'Wow,' she said. 'Will the bomb disposal people come out tonight?'

'Yes. They'll work through the night if needs be. Don't worry. I'll keep you posted.'

'Why do they pick on me, sir?'

'Because you are part of my team. They will do anything to weaken the organisation that is hell bent on stopping them. And you are part of that organisation.'

'Oh dear,' Flora said.

Then Angel said, 'You *are* hell bent on stopping them from killing and robbing, aren't you?'

'Of course I am, sir.'

* * *

It was midnight when the bomb disposal unit arrived at Flora Carter's house. It was an army unit consisting of three men. They began work straight away and by 6 a.m. the following morning they had disarmed the bomb, removed it from the car, taken it to a nearby piece of waste ground and destroyed it.

Flora Carter didn't expect to sleep that night but she did snatch a few hours between 2 and 5 a.m. When she heard the controlled explosion she was overjoyed and at 7 a.m. she brought the three brave workers mugs of tea.

'Will I be able to drive to work now?' she asked the officer in charge.

'Not yet, miss,' he said.

'Oh. Will you be long?'

'We still need to check over the car for any booby traps. I don't think there are any but we need to be certain. I should think we'll be away from here by nine o'clock.'

Flora was disappointed. 'Well, I'll have to be leaving soon.'

'We'll leave your car safe and I'll put your keys through your letterbox, if that's all right?'

* * *

It was a cold, wet and windy morning at the bus stop on the dark, stark, open country road for those waiting for the bus to work or shop in Bromersley.

At 8.05 a.m. there were only six women waiting for the 8.10 bus. As the minutes ticked away more people arrived from all directions creating a considerable gathering at the bus stop of twenty-five or thirty mostly young women.

A minute or two after that, a few more people arrived, including a woman in a green hat and carrying a carrier bag. It was Bridget Dalrymple.

'Good morning, everybody,' she said in a loud Irish twang. 'God bless you all.'

'Good morning,' the small voice of one tiny woman said. Nobody else replied and a few looked away.

Bridget Dalrymple waited for a minute. Then she said:

'The good book says, *Forget not to show love to strangers: for thereby some have entertained angels.* Wonderful thought, now, isn't it?'

The few passengers near her slipped away to a different part of the queue. Some of the remainder looked down at their wet shoes.

A few moments later, ten more people arrived. Among them was DS Flora Carter cosily wrapped up in a raincoat with a hood — protection against the wind.

Suddenly, the bus headlights could be seen approaching on the open country road, cutting its way through the rain and mist. The passengers saw it and became animated. They straightened up and shuffled around for a good position to access the bus.

It momentarily disappeared as the road dipped. Then its warm, amber lights came into sight. Silver arrows of rain crossed the bus's headlights diagonally.

It didn't seem that it was going to stop until it was almost at the bus stop.

Then a woman was squeezed and then pushed out of the crowd towards the nearside wheel of the bus. She landed face down on the sodden road. Her handbag went flying. The driver saw her and with a slight skid of the wheels and squeal of the brakes, he stopped the bus centimetres from the woman's head.

The driver jumped down from the cab and dashed round the bus to see if the woman was injured.

He turned her over by a shoulder.

It was Flora Carter.

He assisted her to her feet.

The passengers crowded round.

The driver said, 'All right, I've got you. Are you all right? What happened?'

'I've got your handbag, love,' an elderly lady said.

Flora Carter rubbed her head and said, 'I'm all right, I think.'

'What happened?'

Her lips tightened with indignation and anger. 'I was pushed,' she said.

Then, over her shoulder through the small crowd she saw a big, black limousine stop along the road about 200 metres away. Bridget Dalrymple appeared on the roadside running towards it. The door in the limousine opened, a man in chauffeur's livery jumped out, assisted her inside and then drove the limousine away from them at speed.

* * *

Later that day, DS Don Taylor knocked at Angel's office door, opened it and stuck his head in. 'Can I see you, sir? Only want a moment of your time.'

'Come in,' Angel said.

'I've got what you wanted. Just delivered. Came in by registered post.'

Angel's face brightened.

'It's got a rubber sucker fitting.'

'Great.' Angel held out his hand. Don dropped the tiny bug into his open palm.

'And the very best of luck, sir.'

'Thank you, Don. Ask Flora to come in, will you?'

A few minutes later, DS Flora Carter arrived.

'Ah, Flora,' he said. 'Come in. Sit down. I've been thinking. We now know where Aaron Penn lives. And we now know that he is at least on nodding acquaintance with Bridget Dalrymple.'

'How do we know that, sir?'

'Old Norman told me that Bennie Jones had mentioned her by name in an affectionate way to Aaron Penn.'

'Can we depend on what Old Norman says, sir?'

'Yes. Absolutely. I've known him years. He's been on the wagon about four. Besides, you can't say "Bridget Dalrymple" if you are drunk.'

Flora smiled weakly.

'As I was saying, as we now know that they know each other, isn't it possible that in that house, gems of information may be dropped from time to time for interested listeners such as ourselves?'

'Do you mean Bridget Dalrymple's address?'

'That. Among other things.'

* * *

The following morning at ten o'clock . . .

A car travelled slowly past the Albury House buildings in Bromersley. Its radio was playing. The volume knob was turned up to the top. It was playing the raucous, screaming recorded voice of a female declaring, 'I'm on fire.' It was accompanied by guitars and drums. The noise shook the car and distressed the ear drums of everybody it passed on the road.

Then suddenly, the car juddered, stopped and began emitting white smoke from around the radiator.

Soon afterwards the radio went dead and the driver, a slim, pretty thirty-something in a denim skirt climbed out of the car and clumsily raised the bonnet. Smoke billowed round the radiator.

She quickly stood back from the raised bonnet and sighed.

It was Detective Sergeant Flora Carter, as tutored by Angel, who looked and acted like a well-to-do dolly daydream. In the waist band of her skirt was a small pocket. In the pocket was the tiny bug.

The production of smoke was from a white grenade as used by the police and the army to provide smokescreens. It was also used on stage and screen to produce special effects. On this occasion, it was being applied to suggest, to anyone who didn't know better, that the car had an overheated radiator.

148

After a few moments watching the smoke, she went to the rear of the car and opened the boot. She rummaged around in there for a minute and then came out with a child's small plastic toy bucket. She held it up to the skyline. It had the capacity of about half a litre.

She took that opportunity to look around at the silent and stark Albury House buildings and then opposite them at the row of terraced houses. The nearest end terraced house was a tall three-storey building which had a window on the top floor of the end wall. As she glanced around to see if she was being observed, she thought she could see the reflection of something light coloured at the window. She kept looking at it. Then suddenly it moved and went away.

It had been the reflection of a face.

Her pulse raced and her chest became hot.

She realised that that window was a perfect place to view what was happening throughout most of the Albury House buildings as well as the roads to, from and around them.

She nodded slightly to convey that the plastic bucket would have to do, then took the bucket and her handbag across the road, round the corner up the service road to the end house and the first back gate. It was an unnecessarily large encumbrance, made of heavy wood hanging off its support by one hinge, the other having rusted away. It had been painted apple green many years ago.

She pressed the sneck, pushed her way through. She went along the concrete pathway through the backyard up three stone steps to the back door.

She took a deep breath, put on her winning smile and knocked on the door.

It was answered by a woman of about fifty. She was slim and must have been beautiful years ago. The wrinkles on her face were now deep-set features. She was wearing a blue plastic overall. She looked down at Flora and smiled.

The door opened directly into a small room used as a kitchen and a dining room. There was a television on a sideboard and a table in the middle of the room.

When Flora saw the table, she decided that the underside of it would be a good place for the bug.

There was the loud sound of cheering crowds from the television. She could see the pictures from the reflection of a mirror over the mantelpiece.

'Sorry to bother you,' Flora began, 'but I was just driving past and my car has broken down—'

The woman frowned and cupped a hand to her ear. 'I can't hear.'

Flora raised her voice and held up the toy bucket and said, 'I need some water for my radiator. Would you kind enough to help me out?'

The woman shouted, 'Sorry, dear. I can't hear you. I'll just turn this down.'

She darted away to the television.

Flora quickly took the bug from her waist band and held it tightly in her hand.

The woman found the remote, pressed the button and the sound went down.

'Now I can hear you, dear,' she said. 'What is it? I put the TV on for my husband, but he's upstairs. It's the football. Mad about it. I'm not interested myself. He asked me to put it on, but look at it. I put it on. Where is he now? Men?'

Flora smiled and repeated her request.

'Of course. Well, don't be shy, dear. Come on in.'

Flora stepped up into the small kitchen–diner and waited in the open doorway.

The woman found a bucket from a cupboard under the sink and began filling it with water. 'You'll be better off with this bigger bucket. You can bring it back when you've finished with it.'

'Thank you,' Flora said as she looked round the little room.

As it was filling with water, the woman went to a door, opened it, put her head round the corner and looked upwards. It was a door leading up the stairs straight from the kitchen.

'Aaron,' she called. 'Are you coming!'

It was Flora's opportunity. She may not get another. She leaned forward, reached out and pressed the rubber sucker on the bug onto the underside of the tabletop. Then straightened up and tried to look innocent.

The woman returned to the sink.

Suddenly, a big man came rushing down the stairs.

'You didn't tell me it had bloody well started,' he said as he pushed himself off the bottom step. He dashed over to the remote and turned up the volume. He was wearing a check shirt and brown trousers held up by stained elastic braces, and sloppy brown slippers.

It was Aaron Penn.

A bolt of icy cold fear ran down Flora's spine.

He saw her. She turned away. He looked her up and down then frowned. Then he sat at the table watching the football.

Her arms and legs turned to goose pimples. She tried to control herself.

Penn took his eyes briefly away from the television and glanced up at Flora again. He said nothing.

Flora looked away. She didn't want to make eye contact. She lifted her head, sucked in her stomach and tightened her lips all to try to look different.

Penn looked thoughtfully back at the television screen.

The woman at the sink turned to Flora and said, 'It's my husband, love. Take no notice.'

Penn looked up. '*What?*!' he roared, glaring at the woman.

She sniffed, and over the cheering of the crowd on the television she shouted sharply, 'I was explaining to this lady—' she broke off — 'turn that television down, when we are talking. *Please.*'

He turned the volume down.

'Thank you,' she said crisply. I was explaining to this lady. Who is it 'as got no manners in this house?'

'What do you mean?' he roared. 'I turned the frigging sound on the television down, didn't I? There's no pleasing you, Clarice.'

The woman turned off the tap, turned to Flora, smiled and said, 'There you are, dear. Take the bucket. Look, I have only half filled it so it's not too heavy.'

Flora said, 'Thank you very much.' She lifted the bucket out of the sink.

'Don't expect '*im* to offer to carry it out for you.'

'What do you mean?' he roared.

'That's all right,' Flora said quickly.

She didn't want Aaron Penn coming any closer to her.

'I can easily manage,' she added.

He glared at his wife. 'There you are,' he said. She says she can easily manage.'

'She *would* say that,' Clarice shouted icily. 'She's been well brung up. She's been taught to be independent — like me. Independent of men, anyway. It wouldn't hurt you to have offered. But you wouldn't think of that. Oh no.'

Flora thought that Aaron Penn had not recognised her. But she wanted to get away from the house because his memory may be on slow burn.

Clarice looked at Flora, grabbed the bucket handle from her and said, 'Come on, dear. I'll give you a hand.'

Flora smiled. 'I really can manage, thank you,' she said.

'Very well, dear,' she said.

Flora took the bucket handle and made for the door. 'I'll bring it back in a few minutes.'

'No rush, dear.'

Flora was much relieved that she was leaving the place. She wanted to put as much space as possible between Aaron Penn and herself. She was relieved that he did not seem to recognise her through what she thought was a very slender disguise.

The smoke grenade had burned out by the time she had reached the car.

In case anyone was watching, she was thinking particularly about the possibility that Penn might be up at the high window, she mimed removing the radiator cap and then mimed the disposing of the water into the radiator by pouring it slowly down the side of it directly onto the road.

Then she went back to the house with the bucket. It was a short journey that troubled her. But she had to appear to finish the operation properly. And there must be no hint that her car didn't break down or that she was a member of the police.

The door was closed. She went up the steps. She could hear the roaring of the football crowd from the television set in the house.

Her heart was racing. She stood and took several deep breaths before she knocked on the door.

It was soon opened by the massive Aaron Penn.

At first she was unable to speak. Her eyebrows shot up. Then, she swallowed, held out the bucket and boldly said, 'I've come to return this. Will you thank your good lady for me?'

The corners of Penn's mouth went upward. He would have called it a smile. Then he stepped backward and opened the door further and said, 'Oh she's right here. Come right in, *Copper!* Come on in. You can thank her yourself.'

Flora flushed up scarlet when she realised she had been identified.

Penn reached out to grab her by the arm.

She pulled back and threw the bucket at his shins.

'Ow,' he yelled. He stumbled over it and fell, trying to get hold of her.

She turned and ran for her life down the steps, through the backyard, dragging the big wooden gate shut behind her.

Penn eventually kicked the bucket out of his way and leaped down the stone steps. He tore the heavy gate off its remaining hinge and discarded it to one side.

Flora raced along the service road, turned on to the main road and across the road to her car.

She was soon inside. She locked the doors. Grabbed her purse to get the car key. It should be there among some coins.

It wasn't there.

She moved the coins up and down the purse. It wasn't there.

Penn reached the car.

His big, red, unshaven, angry face briefly glared at her as he yanked hard the door handle.

'Let me in, you bitch,' he bawled. 'Let me in.'

The car rocked violently.

Flora's mouth dropped open. She raised her eyebrows.

There were a few rattles.

She gasped and grabbed hold of the steering wheel for balance.

The open purse, coins and paper money went flying . . . some landed on her lap, the next seat, the rubber mat . . .

She was breathing heavily. Her face had changed to a ghastly white.

She looked down.

Something on the floor shone brightly.

It *was* the ignition key.

She reached down to the rubber mat.

She sighed and made a slight cry of triumph.

The car started first press.

'Thank God.'

Penn bawled more expletives at her as he hammered his fists heavily on the car driver's window.

He grabbed the door handle again. He rocked the car. And again, And again. Then the handle came off in his hand. He threw it away.

Flora looked away from him as she pressed hard on the accelerator.

Penn's face and fists quickly slid out of view.

She heard a few bangs and noises from the roof and rear of the car as she pulled away. She couldn't guess how much damage Penn had done to the bodywork of the car, but she was away, free. She sighed with relief.

She drove the car as fast as she could, disregarding all speed limits and not yet deciding where to go.

But she had only a short reprieve.

Suddenly, she saw a big, horny hand gripping the wing mirror and an arm down the driver's window from the roof of the car. Then she saw Penn's hair and eyes looking at her upside down through the windscreen. His staring eyes suggested that he was far from being comfortable. He seemed to be precariously positioned across the roof, anchored by a wing mirror at one side of the car. Some jerky driving from her would easily dislodge him and throw him off the roof with possible severe injuries or death. She also realised, however, that whenever she stopped he would be the first person to be with her.

Her heart began to beat rapidly and loudly again.

She had a throbbing sound in her ears.

She kept her eyes on the road and tried not to look into Penn's staring gaze. She would have to keep up a good speed to keep him holding on tight.

When she reached a stretch of straight, open road, she called up Angel on her phone. She told him what had happened and conveyed her present situation.

It was so pleasant to hear his voice. She discovered then that she could breathe normally.

Angel quickly devised a plan and told her what to do.

She sighed with relief.

She travelled along the ring road for a short distance, took the filter road to the town centre and then on to the police station.

She drove relatively fast up the last hill because she expected Penn would be disconcerted when he saw where she was heading.

She drove the car into the police car park, bounced round the corner and was relieved to see Angel, Scrivens (armed with a Heckler and Koch submachine gun) and four other uniformed officers waiting for her and her passenger.

Angel waved her into a parking space obviously prepared for her.

She slowly came to a stop.

Aaron Penn saw the reception party and lowered his head.

Angel reached out and dragged him off the roof of the car by the scruff of the neck.

THIRTEEN

'No comment,' Penn repeated.

Angel wiped his hand across his chin and said, 'You know, Mr Penn, you can't keep saying "no comment" to every question I put to you.'

'Excuse me, Inspector,' said Eugene Bloom, the small, well-dressed solicitor sitting opposite Angel at the table. 'But may I respectfully point out to you that, of course, my client *can* keep saying "no comment" to your questions.'

Angel sniffed and said, 'You are absolutely correct, Mr Bloom. But if he says only that in court, where he is most certainly heading, he may very well be found to be guilty of everything that is thrown at him, including contempt of court. And he would never, ever smell fresh air again.'

'But he doesn't *have* to go into the witness box,' Bloom said triumphantly.

Angel smiled. 'Don't you believe that the jury would think that highly suspicious? And you know very well that if Mr Penn does *not* go in the witness box, all the other witnesses, defendants and barristers can say what they like about him and he has no personal redress whatsoever.'

Bloom said, 'I would respectfully remind you, Inspector Angel, that this is not a high court with a judge and barristers. Another day, another time, perhaps Mr Penn will want to say something different.'

Angel's top lip tightened against his teeth. He was not pleased. 'In such a case, I would see to it that this hindrance to investigation by the police is duly brought to the attention of the court,' he said. 'It is wasting police time which is another charge that can be brought against him.'

Penn shuffled uncomfortably and with a jerk of the head indicated that he wanted to speak to Bloom privately.

Bloom nodded in response then turned to Angel. 'My client wants to speak to me privately, Inspector.'

Angel smiled inwardly. 'Of course.'

Then for the benefit of the tape, he said, 'Interview of Aaron Penn with Mr Bloom by DS Carter and DI Angel stopped briefly to allow discussion between solicitor and client.'

Angel and Carter stood up and made for the door.

They stood outside and waited.

Carter said, 'How do you think it's going, sir?'

'Not sure,' Angel said. 'The witnesses are mostly ourselves — police. Juries prefer to have the facts from people like themselves . . . we'll have to see.'

Bloom opened the door and said, 'Ready, Inspector.'

Angel and Carter returned and the interview continued.

Angel looked at Penn and said, 'Let's revert to my previous question. What do you know about Bridget Dalrymple?'

Penn looked down at the tabletop and eventually said, 'Who?'

Angel shook his head angrily then he said, 'In the absence of the other thug who is up for murder, what—'

Bloom's face went scarlet as he interrupted the detective.

'*Inspector Angel!*' he snapped. 'The question infers that my client *is* a thug, whereas he is a perfectly respectable citizen and you have no evidence to suggest otherwise. I must insist on an instant retraction of that phrase.'

Angel ran his hand across his mouth and said, 'What exactly do you want me to say? Do want me to say that *this* client is not a thug and that your other client, Bennie Jones, *is* a thug? Or that *this* client is a thug and that Bennie Jones is *not* a thug? Or that Aaron Penn and Bennie Jones are *both* thugs? You know that I can only speak the truth.'

Bloom sighed heavily and gritted his teeth. Eventually he said, 'Just say that neither of the two men are thugs.'

'I can't say that, Mr Bloom,' Angel said. 'I *can* say that evidence of dishonest actions and brutality by Penn and Jones against ordinary, innocent citizens has not yet been admitted as evidence, but will follow shortly.'

Bloom swallowed uncomfortably and said, 'If that is accepted, you must say that that both men claimed that there was no truth in the accusations.'

'Very well.'

Angel nodded then turned back to Aaron Penn and said, 'Now then, what is the address of Bridget Dalrymple?'

'Don't know,' Penn said.

'Well,' Angel began, 'where does she hang out? Does she go to a particular pub or club, or has she a special friend?'

'Not that I know of.'

'Does she go regularly to a particular shop or supermarket?'

'No.'

'She's got to eat and sleep. Does she live or stay where someone caters for her? Like a guest house, a hotel or a caravan?'

Penn put his open hands out, palms upwards and said, 'Nar. She doesn't live like that.'

Angel frowned then said, 'You're not going to tell me she lives out in a wood somewhere?'

'No. She doesn't live *anywhere*,' Penn said impatiently.

Angel frowned then said, 'What do you mean she doesn't live anywhere? She's got to live somewhere.'

There was a long pause while Angel waited for an answer.

Penn wiped his moist forehead on his coat sleeve then said, 'It's difficult. I can't tell you any more.'

* * *

It was early on Monday morning . . .

Angel looked at his watch, 'I'll have to go, sweetheart.'

'You've plenty of time,' Mary said. 'Besides that, you're your own boss aren't you?'

Angel smiled. 'No I'm not,' he said.

'Well, you know what I mean.'

He finished the last drop of tea, put down the cup, pushed back his chair, leaned over, gave Mary a kiss and left the table.

He dashed into the hall, grabbed his old overcoat, came back into the kitchen and began to put it on.

'And you will be careful, won't you?' she said. 'It's been pretty scary since that ghastly kidnapping of Mr Scrivens.'

'Don't be worrying about me. I can look after myself. And we did get Ted Scrivens free, you know — look at him now. He is in great health. It's made a better copper out of him.'

Mary said, 'I wouldn't want to go what he went through. I don't want anybody sticking needles into me.'

Angel momentarily flinched at what she had said, but quickly forced a smile and said, 'It'll never happen to you, Sunshine.'

Mary's face changed. 'Do you *have* to go in today, darling? Couldn't you take the day off?'

'You know I can't, not when I'm so far on with a murder case . . . particularly at such short notice. Besides I've got an important interview which must be made while the witness is "hot". You know that. You'll be all right. You can always get me on the phone. If you're in trouble phone me. You know that. Now I *must* go.'

She stood up, put her arms round his neck, and gave him a long kiss.

He smiled, squeezed her hand and rushed out.

She followed him to the door, watched him drive the BMW out of the garage onto the road and leave for the police station.

FOURTEEN

'It's time we cleared up the rest of the Madigan gang,' Angel said, pulling his chair closer to his desk.

DS Flora Carter said, 'There is only Bridget Dalrymple that we know of. Now that Penn has been charged. Of course, there's the little man . . . the painter . . . the one who drives her around. May be others we don't yet know about.'

He wrinkled his nose. 'If we can capture and charge them, the small fry will disappear into the woodwork. We must find Bridget Dalrymple and we can call this case closed. Did you check all the mobile telephone calls made by the victims over the past three months?'

'Yes, sir,' Flora said. 'And there was nothing . . . nothing involving crime . . . any sort of crime in each one that I could detect.'

'And have their living quarters, wherever they might be over the last three months, been thoroughly searched?'

'Absolutely, yes.'

'Well, have we sufficient evidence to be able to charge Bridget Dalrymple for all the murders?'

'Possibly, all of them except maybe Rodney Pertwee,' Flora said.

Angel tapped his pen against his chin then said, 'It is probably possible to compare the MO of those murdered with that of Pertwee and thus bring a charge against her for *his* murder also.'

'But where is she?' Flora said. 'She must have gone to ground.'

Angel sighed and held out his arms, palms upwards and said, 'People like her don't go to ground. She likes to show off. She likes to be heard. She likes to be seen. She seems to prefer witnesses. What sort of a murderer is that? I've never come across such a case where the murderer goes out of their way to be seen by witnesses.'

Flora sat there not attempting an answer. She sat there pursing her lips and breathing out a long length of air . . . waiting for Angel to say more.

'Have you searched Aaron Penn's house?' he said.

'I've sent Sean Donohue over to Ted Scrivens who is getting a team together now . . . everybody we can spare.'

'Have you interviewed Penn's wife?'

'Clarice Penn. Yes, sir. But she wasn't at all cooperative. She didn't say anything incriminating.'

'Have you got a warrant?' Angel said.

'Yes, sir,' Flora said. 'Got it signed last night.'

'I'll come with you, ' Angel said.

* * *

Out on the police vehicle car park, Angel turned round to the four uniformed men and the three in plain clothes and said, 'You all know that we are looking for an Irish woman known as Bridget Dalrymple. She is the head of what is left of the Madigan gang. She is a serial murderer. The house we are going to turn over was until yesterday the home of Aaron Penn. He was a prominent member of the gang. So this search is particularly important. Remember, I want anything brought to my attention if it is a weapon, explosives, a syringe, obviously any drugs, letters, strange notes on scraps of paper, exorbitant amounts of cash, anything at all you think unusual, or anything out of context. Now let's do a quick, efficient job and let's get the remnants of this horrible gang finally behind bars.'

* * *

Six PCs, DI Angel and DS Carter in three cars arrived outside the front door of Aaron Penn's house.

Angel instructed two of the constables to go round to the back door.

Meanwhile, the police crowded round Angel on the front step. He knocked hard with the doorknocker and waited. There was no answer.

He tried again.

Angel looked at Flora Carter and said, 'There's something funny going on. I'm going round the back. Keep up the racket. Force your way in if you have to. There should only be Clarice Penn in there.'

Angel went round the back of the house and saw immediately that there was a ruckus in progress.

Clarice Penn was leaning with her back against the yard wall in a short-sleeved blouse showing her many tattoos of threatening snakes and other dangerous animals in challenging poses. She was red in the face and perspiring profusely.

Her mousey-coloured hair flopped over her face some of the time. She frequently blew it, and when she had hands free pushed it back from her eyes. She was lunging out with one fist at one of the two young policemen who was attempting to fit her up with handcuffs behind her back. It seemed they had managed to cuff her left wrist but could not manage the right. Then Angel saw the other PC on the floor, looking dazed with his nose bleeding.

Angel rushed round to the service road and through the gap where the gate had been and went to the aid of the PC.

'Get away,' Clarice Penn yelled. 'Leave off, you buggers!'

But the two men persisted and the handcuffs were eventually fitted.

When that was done, she struggled to try to get out of them. She pulled and pushed in all directions for a time. Then, exhausted she stopped struggling.

'You rotten sods,' she yelled. 'This is police harassment! Police harassment, nothing less. Help. Help. HELP!!'

'Mrs Penn!' Angel shouted. Then in a more moderate tone he said, 'Mrs Penn, you can't win, you know. There are six more officers at your front door. And this ruckus could be called resisting arrest. And there's assaulting a police office, withholding information . . . All this could cost you a fine and maybe imprisonment.'

'I don't care,' she said. 'Anyway, what more do you want? You've got my husband locked up. And you're running riot through my house as if it was a bloody supermarket. I've told you all I know.'

'Not quite,' he said. 'Come on, let's get inside.'

Clarice Penn turned round and with her arms strapped uncomfortably behind her back she mounted the steps at the back door. Angel followed her. It was straight into the kitchen.

He closed the back door. Assisted the woman to a seat at the kitchen table and then sat down there himself.

It was a noisy place to be.

There were police in and out of the rooms busy tapping the walls and listening, checking the loft, unscrewing suspicious panels, upping loose floorboards . . . giving the house a thorough search.

Flora Carter was passing the open door from the tiny hall into the kitchen and, seeing Angel and Mrs Penn, leaned inside and waited for Angel to look her way. Then she said, 'Excuse me, sir. We had to force our way in.'

Angel nodded and said, 'Carry on, Flora. I want to have a little talk with Mrs Penn. Just for a few minutes. Will you organise the team to search this room last? And close that door on your way out?'

'Righto, sir,' she said.

As soon as the door was closed, Mrs Penn said, 'I've nothing to say. I've said all I have to say until my brief gets here.'

Angel thought a moment then said, 'Did you know how long you'll probably get in prison?'

She sat down in the chair opposite him. 'I know I was told not to talk without a brief.'

'Quite right,' he said. 'But this is an off-the-record chat. Nothing is being recorded or written down. There's just you and me.'

'You know, I'm not afraid of you.'

'I wouldn't want you to be, Clarice,' Angel said. 'You don't mind if I call you Clarice. It is your name, isn't it? You can call me Michael.'

'I do mind. It is Mrs Penn. And I will call you Pig.'

Angel pursed his lips. He was thinking. He reckoned he had a real tough nut to crack here.

Then he had an idea.

'Very well. Is there anything you want to ask me?'

'No, I don't think so,' she said. Then she said, 'Yes, there is. Yes. Do you really think my husband will be found guilty of anything and if so, how long will he get?'

Angel lowered his head and shook it slightly then looked up and said, 'He'll be found of guilty of several murders. I cannot see him getting less than thirty years.'

She sighed. '*Thirty* years?'

Angel nodded. 'Afraid so.'

'Is there anything . . . anything that would make his sentence any less?' Clarice said.

'Nothing. Only abundantly assisting the police with their inquiries. But I won't lie to you. A deal cannot be struck. Before the trial, the judge is officially informed, if any, and how much assistance was given and if any saving of time aided the police with the case. He alone decides if and how much a reduction should be made to the sentence. Usually they are very fair.'

Clarice Penn looked down at the floor. She rolled her shoulders, trying to get comfortable, and said, 'Are these handcuffs really necessary?'

'If you behave yourself, I'll unlock one of them while we are here but I will have to fit you up again when we leave. We take them off completely when we get to the police station.'

Clarice Penn pulled a sour face. 'Undo them,' she said, standing up and leaning slightly forward. 'I'd promise the world to get these off.'

Angel pulled the key out of his pocket and released her left wrist.

'Aaaaaah,' she said with relief. The handcuffs dangled noisily as she rubbed her wrists. She sat down and exercised the hand and wrist that had been constricted.

Angel pocketed the key then sat down.

Clarice Penn eventually brought both hands onto the table, the handcuffs rattling at every movement.

Angel said, 'Are you in any way uncomfortable now?'

'Only worried about what you want to know that you think I can tell you.'

'You can tell me about Bridget Dalrymple.'

Clarice Penn blinked then said, 'Bridget Dalrymple? She's a leprechaun, isn't she? In real life, she doesn't exist.'

Angel rubbed his chin. 'But she *does* exist,' he said. 'I've met her. And I believe that Bridget Dalrymple and your husband were in Mad Doug Madigan's gang. And that she took over when he was caught. Where does she live?'

'Under a bloody toadstool, doesn't she?'

Angel sighed noisily and turned away.

'She doesn't live anywhere,' she said. 'I told you, in real life she doesn't exist.'

Angel's face muscles tightened. Then he suddenly spoke out loudly.

'She recently murdered several good living people in front of real live ordinary people,' he said. 'We have signed statements, we have a dozen or so witnesses, so I know she exists. Where can I find her? I have to find her before she murders again.'

'I have no idea what you're talking about,' she said. 'And if I did know, I don't see why I should tell you.'

'If you have any love or merely consideration for your fellow man and his family, you *should* tell me. If you don't want to tell me then tell some other policeman. Don't you realise that if you know anything at all and she murders again, that you could have prevented it. And it will be on your conscience for the rest of your life.'

Clarice Penn thought a few moments then said, 'Nar.'

FIFTEEN

In the car on his way to the station, Angel shook his head and said, 'Flora, it's without doubt the most baffling case I have ever had. We've a murderer who likes to murder in public and is described by those who know her as a leprechaun, or they say she does not exist. And nobody knows where she lives or where she goes.'

Flora said, 'She must have a bed somewhere. Or a chair.'

Angel said, 'Or a nail to hang her vest on.'

* * *

It was 5.30 p.m.

Angel yawned and pushed himself back from his desk.

It was dark outside. Winter was coming. He wrinkled his nose. He put a pencil between the pages of the report he had been reading as a bookmark and closed it up.

He had been reading all the reports in the earlier days of the case, hoping to find an avenue he had not explored. Or anything else that would throw light on the case. He couldn't see where he had missed anything.

The phone rang.

He reached out for it and said, 'Angel.'

'Good afternoon, Inspector, this is Maurice Mountjoy of Mountjoy Films. Can I talk to you a minute or so?'

'Of course,' he said. 'Have you some evidence to offer in connection with this case?'

'No. It's not that. Although I might have.'

'When do you want to come round?'

'Actually, I am at the front of your police station. Now, if that's possible. It's very important.'

'All right. Wait there, and I'll come and bring you through to my office.'

Angel met up with him at the door and brought him through to his office. Angel gestured towards a chair opposite him over the desk. Mountjoy slumped down into it and looked down at the floor thoughtfully.

'Now then, Mr Mountjoy. What did you want to tell me?' Angel said.

The man did not reply immediately.

Angel asked, 'Are you in trouble?'

'I am afraid so.'

'How can I help?'

Mountjoy said, 'It will not have escaped your notice that the murders in Bromersley over the past few weeks have been key personnel in my employ.'

Angel nodded.

Mountjoy continued. 'I have tried to replace them . . . but it has not been easy replacing people of the quality of Edward Schulz, Rodney Pertwee and Samantha Rock, and a cinematographer of the genius of James Lee. But the murders have not stopped. And I can't go on forever. Now I have reached the end of the line. I have signed contracts with second-class replacements which means I have now to begin payment to them and I haven't shot a frame of anybody. Also I have had to pay them and all the other smaller parts and the crew these past few weeks to keep them together for when we *can* get shooting. But I can't go on any further.'

He stopped as if he was marshalling his next words.

Angel said, 'What can I do?'

Mountjoy smiled sadly then looked down at his hands and said, 'Now the bank has foreclosed on me and so I have no option but to go into liquidation. They have also given me notice to vacate my house in fourteen days. By tomorrow, it will be all over the national papers.'

Angel said, 'What bank was that?'

'The Great Northern Bank,' he said, spitting out each word angrily. 'That means I won't be able to get enough credit to buy a lollipop.'

'I'm very sorry to hear that, Mr Mountjoy. Does this mean that you have no income?'

'Not quite. We have small pensions, my wife and I, that will just about pay for three meals a day and a bed at night . . . so we shall not starve. I am advising you because my wife and I are leaving Bromersley tomorrow. We shall return to London and . . . start again.'

'How is your wife taking all this?'

'She's very strong, you know. It's amazing how she has responded to all this, but she is looking forward to returning to London.'

Angel said, 'We'll be sad to lose you and hope you will find a happy solution to the problem. You'll let me have a contact address when you get settled?'

'Of course.'

'You never know, we might need you back as a witness.'

Mountjoy shook his head then angrily said, 'I hope not.'

* * *

At home that evening as they were finishing supper, Angel told Mary about the plight of the film producer, Mountjoy, and ended by saying, 'Fancy anybody preferring London to Bromersley.'

Mary looked up and, as she poured cream over the apple pie, said, 'That's not what I heard . . . and, by the way, I went to have my hair done today and you've never mentioned a word about it.'

Angel looked across at her. 'It looks great,' he said. But you always look great. Why would I comment on it?'

As she passed the cream over to him, Mary shook her head knowingly and at the same time smiled. Then she said, 'There are millions of people who prefer London. There's the shops, theatres, museums . . . there are lots of good things there.'

'What was that you heard?' Angel said.

'Can't remember . . . Oh yes, at the hairdresser's . . . Margaret Mountjoy, his wife, was there, having her roots done. And I heard her tell Cynthia Benson that they are going to South America. And they are flying to Rio de Janeiro tomorrow.'

Angel frowned. 'For a holiday?'

'Oh yes. It would be a holiday . . . a cruise, I suppose? I don't really know . . .'

'Expensive,' Angel said thoughtfully.

Then suddenly, he put down his cutlery, stood up and said, 'What's Margaret Mountjoy look like?'

'She's all right.'

'What's she look like? How tall is she?'

'Average. Average for a woman. Why?'

'Does she talk with an Irish accent?'

'No. I haven't seen her standing. She was having her hair done, not trying on a coat. And anybody can talk with an Irish accent. What's the matter?'

'Maurice Mountjoy said that they were going to *London* tomorrow. And he will be looking for a job.'

Mary said, 'So what? She'd be showing off. She'd think nobody would check on her. I mean, going on a cruise to South America sounds a million times better than seeing the sights in London freezing in an open-top bus touring round the streets.'

'Mountjoy played the hard-up card and said that he was leaving for London looking for a *job*. I've *got* to go out.'

He left the apple pie and cream and stood up.

Mary's face dropped. Her eyes flashed. She looked at the grandfather clock. It was 7 p.m. And said, 'At *this* time?'

'Won't be long, love,' he said.

He rushed into the hall and grabbed his hat and coat. He went back into the kitchen, gave her a kiss on the cheek and said again, 'Won't be long.'

On his way out through the hall, he swiped an arrangement of flowers leaving the vase and water behind. Then he went out into the night. He backed the car out of the garage and was soon on the ring road.

He knew the Mountjoys' house although he had never been inside. It was in Bromersley on Seeforth Road which was made up of architect-designed houses and bungalows, built in the twenties.

He stopped the car outside their house. He opened the boot and wrapped the flowers in brown paper. Then he opened the garden gate and walked down the garden path.

The moon illuminated the path to the front door. As he stood there, he became aware of some movement in the bushes at the other side of the lawn. He turned to see the silhouette of a man in boots, baggy trousers and overcoat holding a garden spade.

'Who is it?' the man said gruffly.

'It's Michael Angel. Is that you, Mr Mountjoy?'

'Ah. Yes, yes, it's me,' he said. 'What can I do for you?'

He didn't sound very pleased.

Angel said, 'I have a small present for you and your wife to see you on your way tomorrow.'

'That's very kind.'

'Doing some gardening?' he said with a grin. 'Not easy in the dark, is it?'

'I want it to be smart for the new owner and besides that, I wanted some fresh air.'

Angel didn't believe him.

'Shall we go in?' Angel said.

Mountjoy was hesitant.

'It's a bit of a muddle. I don't know what my wife will say. As you know, we are off tomorrow.'

He opened the door and in the hall was met by a neat pile of luggage comprising two large suitcases and then ten or so new silver matching cases of different shapes and sizes all labelled. He squeezed past them holding up the flowers and managed a glance at one of the labels. It read: *PURPLE CLOUD LINE, SS MELANIE, MR & MRS M. MOUNTJOY AND MR E. MOUNTJOY, RIO DE JANEIRO, BRAZIL. TO BE COLLECTED.*

Mountjoy followed him. He saw Angel reading a label.

They both stood together in the hall.

Angel looked at him and said, 'I thought you said you were going to London?'

Mountjoy pursed his lips then said, 'We are, we are going there on business.'

Angel pointed to the huge pile of luggage behind him and said, 'Do you think you'll have enough clean vests?'

Mountjoy looked at Angel up and down.

'I'll see if I can find my wife,' he said. 'You won't keep her long, will you? She has such a lot to do.'

'No. Just like to meet her.'

He turned and went up the stairs.

Angel quickly looked through the half-open door of the nearest room. It seemed to be the drawing room. It was clean but untidy. A grand piano with photographs in frames but mostly flattened stood on the shiny top . . . many were on the polished oak floor . . . silver frames, loose photographs amidst broken glass. Angel saw a loose, postcard-sized, clear head-and-shoulders photograph of Mountjoy. He quickly snatched it up, slipped it into his pocket, returned to the hall, pulled the door to the position it had been in and tried to look innocent.

'She was still packing, would you believe?' Mountjoy said as he descended the stairs.

A pretty, diminutive woman following him said, 'I would love to meet Inspector Angel. I have heard so much about him.'

Mountjoy turned round to her and said, 'This gentleman is Inspector Angel, Margaret. Inspector, this is my wife, Margaret. He heard that we are going to Rio *for a holiday*.'

Margaret smiled widely and shook Angel's outstretched hand. Then dutifully said, 'Yes, Inspector, we are going to Rio *on business*.'

Angel knew that it wasn't exactly the truth. Also, he was disappointed. Margaret Mountjoy was a good ten centimetres too short and far too attractive to be Bridget Dalrymple. Also she had small hands and a high-pitched voice. It had been a crazy idea. Crazy. He might just as well go back home. He handed over the flowers, wished them well and took his leave.

* * *

It was still dark outside when Angel woke up from a deep sleep with a start. He looked at the clock. He could just see the dial. It said 4.45 a.m.

He didn't know what had awakened him. It wasn't Mary. He looked at her fondly. She was quietly enjoying a peaceful sleep.

He lay there quietly listening. He waited sixty seconds or more, wondering what he must be worrying about. Of course there were the letters threatening to murder him that had a Harrogate postmark. When Angel's mind was not on anything else, it always remembered the threat which says that the murderer is someone he trusts and meets often. He must keep his eyes and ears open at all times. He wondered who would send such a letter?

He tried to return to sleep but he was unavoidably thinking about the Bridget Dalrymple case. Something was niggling him. But he couldn't put his finger on it. He gently unravelled Mary's arm which was tangled with his and sat up. He didn't want to disturb her.

Then suddenly he remembered . . . he hadn't asked and wasn't told what Mountjoy was really doing in the garden with a spade in the dark. Mountjoy implied that the house was sold and that he was keeping down the weeds to welcome the new owners . . . And that he was doing it the night before they leave for Rio?

It was not believable. It was ridiculous.

176

But this story was not *all* made up. He had seen luggage actually labelled for Rio.

He gently lifted the duvet, turned, put his feet on the floor and sat on the edge of the bed.

What Mountjoy had been doing with the spade suddenly felt important. You don't pull buttercups or chickweed out with a spade. You frequently plant seeds and saplings and flowers. You dig holes . . . you bury things . . . bury things?

If he was lucky, he could get to Mountjoy's house at first light, before any earth turned last night had dried out.

He must take a spade. He had one in his garden hut.

* * *

He parked his car on the road a few doors away from Mountjoy's house.

The sky was becoming much brighter. He had timed it just right. It was almost seven o'clock.

He took the spade from out of the boot of his car, walked quietly up to Mountjoy's house. He looked at the windows. Some of the upstairs rooms had curtains drawn. There were no lights. It all seemed quiet. He must not disturb them. He quietly opened the gate and went straight across the lawn up to the part of the border where the man was gardening when he had first arrived last night.

Angel pulled out a torch and looked closely along the flower border.

There was nothing untoward to be seen. The soil was dull grey that suggested it had not been disturbed for a while. He went up to the bush where Mountjoy had been standing. He shone the torch behind it. The soil was a dark brown in places and various other shades from black to grey across a strip.

Eureka!

His pulse raced in anticipation.

The area seemed to be quite a size: two metres by seventy-five centimetres approximately . . . about the size of a body. He didn't fancy finding a body and having another murder case to solve before Christmas!

He pushed the spade down hard in the earth. At about twenty centimetres down it felt as if he had met something spongy. He cleared away the soft soil with his hands and discovered a black cotton-like material showing. He pulled at it. It wouldn't give. He cleared more soil. It seemed like a body. He cleared more soil and pulled at it. Eventually, he revealed a woman's black skirt. He dug feverishly and pulled out a woman's overcoat, a white blouse, stockings and a pair of black low-heeled women's shoes. The size of the shoes seemed huge for a woman. But, as yet, there was no body.

He returned to the dig and found a polythene bag showing through the earth. He pulled it out and shook off the soil. Inside he found a cigar box half-full of sticks of theatrical make-up, a woman's wig of brown hair greying and a woman's green hat. There were a few stray hairs on the lining of the wig. Angel was careful not to disturb them. Underneath was the strangest garment — if that's what it was. It comprised four flesh-coloured linen pads sewn together with long tapes. When he arranged it on the lawn he saw that it was a sort of undergarment or padding that would apparently change the figure of a man into that of a woman.

Angel was excited. He was now satisfied that Maurice Mountjoy was indeed the elusive Bridget Dalrymple, serial murderer. He smoothed out the border to make it look undisturbed, glanced at his watch. It was eight o'clock. He looked on the lawn at what he had uncovered then looked across at Mountjoy's house. All was still quiet. That was good.

He wanted to transport these objects to the police station as soon as possible. He needed Don Taylor of SOCO to confirm the ownership of them scientifically. Also he wanted confirmation that the DNA of the owner of the stray hairs on the wig were Mountjoy's. These items would prove to be damning exhibits at his trial.

He collected the items he had uncovered in his arms and took them down to his car. Then while he was in the car, he took out his phone and tapped in his home number to speak to Mary. He had to break the news to her.

When he had told her about Maurice Mountjoy and Bridget Dalrymple being one and the same, she said, 'What was his motive?'

'It was obvious,' he said 'I should have noticed. It was an insurance scam. Mountjoy received a huge payment when Rodney Pertwee, world-renowned actor, was shot dead, and other huge payments when actor Samantha Rock, a Hollywood beauty, Edward Schultz, UK and US director of a list of Oscar-winning films, and cinematographer James Lee, master of lighting and creator of the right shot, were murdered. The biggest payment of all was made when production of the film was cancelled. He's got away with millions.'

'That's marvellous, darling. Aren't you clever?'

He felt a bit silly when Mary said that.

'I'm ringing to tell you I'll be late — too late for lunch and very late for dinner. I have to find him and arrest him, and I don't know where he is.'

'See you when I see you then, love,' she said. 'Be careful. Goodbye.'

He cancelled the call and tapped in DS Flora Carter's home number.

'Hello.'

'Flora? It's Michael Angel. Sorry to bother you so early. It's an emergency. Will you come to Maurice Mountjoy's house as soon as possible? He is the Bridget Dalrymple character and is very dangerous, so be wary. He almost certainly will be armed and I am not. Park your car behind my car.'

It began to dawn on Angel that Mountjoy posing as Bridget Dalrymple and blatantly murdering the stars and key members of the team of the film, in front of so many responsible eyewitnesses, could simply disappear forever by simply burying the disguise. Thereafter, convinced that she was the guilty one, police forces throughout the world may continue looking for a Bridget Dalrymple forever.

It was nine o'clock. He went up the street and glanced up at the windows, again the curtains had not been drawn back. In fact, there didn't seem to be any life in the house at all. Considering they were planning to go to Rio de Janeiro you would have expected them to be making an early start . . .

Angel's hand dived into his pocket and pulled out his phone. He scrolled down to Mountjoy's home number, clicked on it, and then it began to ring. It rang and rang and rang and rang and rang . . .

Angel's head dropped. He shook his head. His mouth dropped open.

Keeping the phone ringing, he raced up the street to Mountjoy's garden, then over the gate to the front door. He rang the bell and banged on the door using the heavy knocker. There was no reply. He tried again and waited . . . and waited. There was still no reply. He looked through the letterbox. The pile of luggage was still there. Of course, that would go later and cheaper as cargo!

Angel breathed out a long lung full of air as he wondered what to do.

Then he suddenly had an idea. He scrolled his phone to Travel Agents. Thankfully, there were only two in Bromersley. He tapped the phone number of one of them. They had never heard of Mountjoy. He gave his thanks and phoned the second. The receptionist at the second answered in the affirmative.

Angel asked to speak to the manager urgently.

The manager said, 'Yes, Inspector, I know Mr Mountjoy. How can I assist the police?'

Angel said, 'This is very urgent. We know that they are emigrating to Rio de Janeiro but have no information about their travel arrangements. We have to get in touch with them. Will you please tell me the details?'

'Just a moment,' the manager said and he put the handset down.

Angel heard the knock and scraping noise it made through the earpiece.

While he waited, Angel wondered where Flora Carter was.

He impatiently tapped repeatedly on the steering wheel with a fist while he gripped the mobile phone very tightly with his other.

Eventually, the manager returned.

'Inspector, the reservation is for a party of three. Maurice Mountjoy, Eric Mountjoy and Margaret Mountjoy. They are leaving the UK today by flight J23, British Airways from Heathrow at 1500 hours. All booked, confirmed and paid for.'

'Thank you,' Angel said with a sigh. He closed his phone. He looked at his watch. It was now 9.55.

Five hours and five minutes.

How on earth could he reach Heathrow in that time? And who was Mr E. Mountjoy?

He pulled out his phone again. He scrolled down to a number and clicked on it. It was answered by a young man.

'Yorkshire Police Helicopter service. Can I help you?'

Angel introduced himself and asked him if he was in a position to help him. He said he was. So Angel gave him a concise version of what it was all about. He had some security to go through and when that was done, the young man said, 'I am Pilot Officer James Keeley. I have some more formalities to go through . . .'

Angel groaned.

'Won't take long,' Keeley said. 'Then I have to take on some juice.'

Angel wasn't pleased and said, 'If we allow this serial murderer to take to the air, he will very likely get away!'

'Inspector Angel, we don't take on board more juice than we need, because it slows us down. I have to pick you up then we have to get to Heathrow. To get back, I can refill at Heathrow. I've got your location in my GPS, of course. But in addition, it'd save us some time if you can get hold of some double-bed-sized white sheets? You need about six.'

Angel was beginning to think his arrest of Mountjoy was impossible.

'I expect so,' he said sourly. 'What for?'

'You're south of here and south of Bromersley, aren't you?' Keeley said. 'With the sheets, make a big white cross on a piece of road, or field or wherever you can. It will make you easier to find and a safe place for me to land. Cheer up, Inspector. Won't be long.'

Keeley ended the call.

Angel closed his phone and growled angrily. And where on earth was DS Carter? And he had six white sheets to find. Where was he going to get them at such short notice?

He remembered that he saw that the Mountjoys' house was still well furnished. He hoped they had six white sheets.

He dashed out of the BMW to Mountjoys' back kitchen window and with a well-covered elbow, jabbed it through a pane. There was tinkle of broken glass tumbling onto kitchen tiles. He reached inside, lifted the handle and opened the window. The house was untidy but most of the furniture seemed to be still there. His first thought was a linen cupboard. But he couldn't find one. Then a linen chest, but he couldn't find one of them either.

He went into the tidiest bedroom. It had a double bed and it was made up. He went into up to it, pulled off the white duvet and the bottom sheet. They were white and absolutely spotless. He did the same in the next two bedrooms and dragged it all onto the landing when he suddenly heard a door close.

It sounded like the front door.

He froze.

He peered over the landing rail. There was nothing to see. He listened. All he could hear was a dog barking a long way away, then the occasional rustle of clothes as the visitor was looking around the downstairs.

Angel gritted his teeth. This was no time to have visitors, especially as he wasn't armed.

Sounded as if the visitor was searching downstairs and presumably then would come upstairs.

Images of who it could be flashed through his mind. That man . . . that person who wrote those poisonous letters posted in Harrogate and was going to murder him had not yet shown his or her hand.

He tightly gripped the landing rail and peered over.

Then he heard a woman's voice call from the bottom of the stairs, 'Hello . . . anybody there?'

It was DS Carter.

He sighed with relief. Then inwardly laughed at himself.

'Flora, will you come up here and take some of these sheets and duvets out to the lawn? Keep them as clean as you can.'

She began to ascend the stairs. She cleared her throat then, disbelieving said, 'You want these sheets and duvets on the lawn?'

'Yes, quick as you can.'

Together they quickly made a white cross on Mountjoy's lawn.

When they had finished, Flora said, 'I hope the pilot will be able to see that.'

Angel said, 'I reckon on a clear day you would be able to see that from Mars.'

He brought Flora up to date with all that happened and then pulled out his phone, he scrolled down to a number and rang it.

It was soon answered.

'Metropolitan Police. Can I help you?' a young man's voice said.

'Detective Inspector Michael Angel of Bromersley Police. Can I speak to the duty officer?'

'Please hold, sir.'

Another voice came on the line.

'DI Spark, duty officer. Can I help you?'

'I hope so,' Angel said. 'Briefly, Inspector, I have a serial murderer from my patch in South Yorkshire on his way to Heathrow Airport. He and his wife and another are intending to emigrate to Rio de Janeiro and they are booked onto flight J23 leaving at 1500 hrs. If he succeeds in leaving the country, you will understand, I may never manage to bring him back. He will get off free as a bird. My sergeant and I hope to be at

Heathrow in an hour or less. We are awaiting the Yorkshire Police helicopter. Could you hold them for us until we get there?'

'Mmmm. I see. Well, we do have a unit at Heathrow. Have you got a warrant for his arrest?' Spark said.

'No. I've only just had evidence to show that he has been committing the murders. I will send you a photograph of him to assist.'

'You might as well. Are they travelling under their own names?'

'Yes. Maurice and Margaret Mountjoy and Mr E. Mountjoy. By the way, they may be armed.'

'So are all our Heathrow officers. I can make no promises, Inspector. We are pulled out of the place with calls on us from all over. And we don't know you. What is your station?'

'Bromersley, it's a market town in South Yorkshire.'

'Bromersley? Isn't that that little one-horse station where that amazing inspector — can't remember his name — always gets his man?'

'Well, er, er, yes, I s'pose . . .' Angel said. 'But he'll lose that record if you don't assist him with this case.'

'Wow!' Spark said. 'We must try and do something then. Trouble is . . . you've no warrant. Hmm. Never mind. Leave it with me.'

He rang off.

Angel turned to Flora, dived into his pocket, pulled out the photograph he had picked up from the floor in Mountjoy's house, handed it to her and said, 'Will you email a copy of that to the Met for the urgent attention of DI Spark?'

SIXTEEN

Angel and Flora were standing on the garden path in Mountjoy's front garden looking up at the clouds.

Angel checked his watch. It was 1.30 p.m.

He shook his head and bit his lower lip. 'Where is it, for goodness' sake?' Angel said. 'It's ninety minutes to when that plane leaves Heathrow.'

'We've got to be patient,' Flora said.

Suddenly, there was one hell of a racket from above as a helicopter came out of the clouds apparently from nowhere.

Angel's jaw dropped open.

The helicopter slowly descended, hovered a few seconds, then gently landed on Mountjoy's lawn. Right on the white cross.

It was much bigger than he had expected and the racket it made seemed even louder.

They rushed across to the helicopter door, Angel opened it, then he shouted out to the young man in the pilot's seat, 'Are you James Keeley?'

He nodded, smiled and shouted, 'Jump in.'

Seconds later they were in the air and heading south.

The journey was uneventful. The noise of the machine made conversation between them difficult.

The pilot got on with his job. He knew that time was important.

Flora sat unhappily wearing her seat belt and making herself as small as she could. She didn't like travelling by air anyway and pointedly avoided looking out of the window.

Angel kept checking his watch and worrying that it was going to be too late to stop the three o'clock plane to Rio.

They landed on the helicopter pad, thanked Keeley and looked round for a sign to the Manager's office, but they couldn't see one. There were crowds of people. They thought it seemed that everybody was busy dashing around going somewhere, but they never saw anybody arrive.

The only fairly stationary character was a PC holding a rifle at his waist and covered in bulletproof clothing.

Angel flashed his warrant card and badge at him. 'Looking for the Manager's office. Can you direct us? It's very urgent.'

He looked around the area first then back at Angel and said, 'Follow me.'

They went up escalators and down escalators, across big halls and through small halls to a waiting room with several doors. One of the doors was designated MANAGER'S OFFICE.

Angel, much relieved, thanked the armed policeman, knocked on the door and walked in.

He was met by a secretary and asked to see the manager.

He briefly explained the situation. But access was denied.

'I'm sorry,' she said, 'but it isn't possible to see the manager at such short notice. I can make an appointment for some time next week . . .'

Angel became aware of a heavy feeling in his stomach.

He sent a note through on the back of his business card. It said, 'Murder of a passenger is imminent if the flight to Rio is not delayed. Must briefly speak with you, please.'

He gave it to the secretary then looked at his watch. It was two fifty-seven. Three minutes to go.

The armed policeman was standing by.

Angel and Flora waited and waited and waited. Angel stood up several times and approached the secretary's desk. Before he could say anything, she shrugged and said, 'There's nothing more I can do.'

The manager came out of his office with Angel's card in his hand. 'What's this all about, Inspector?' he said. 'I am concerned that flights anywhere from here are absolutely safe and leave on time. I cannot delay them for any other reasons. If I did, I would never get any planes off the ground.'

Angel flashed his warrant card and said, 'But the man is a serial murderer escaping with millions of pounds. I am asking you simply to delay the take-off for a few minutes, that's all.'

'You can phone to Rio ahead of his landing and have their police do what's necessary,' the manager said.

'He's a very slippery customer,' Angel said.

'Why leave all this till today? Why didn't you come yesterday? You could have arrested him in the waiting area. Better than leaving it all to the very last minute.'

'I didn't have the evidence yesterday,' Angel said.

'Book a seat on tomorrow's flight. You should be able to catch up with him. You know, Inspector, I cannot disturb the other passengers on the plane, the crew and the staff at the other end, merely to make your life easier. Now, if you will excuse me, I have a great number of matters to attend to.'

The manager turned and went back into the shelter of his office.

Angel felt that he had been battered round the head by a giant with a double-decker bus.

Flora didn't know what to say to him.

The armed PC had been watching them from a short distance. He came up to them and said, 'What's wrong?'

Angel said, 'The manager doesn't want to know. He's allowing a serial murderer with millions of stolen pounds to escape to Rio.'

'What did he say?' the PC asked.

'He said that his priorities are to see that flights are absolutely safe and leave on time. He obviously doesn't make any allowance for any other emergency. But once Maurice Mountjoy hits the ground in Rio, he and his wife and Eric Mountjoy — whoever he is — will assume other identities and be lost among the hundreds at the airport and many millions of people in the world. They may never be brought to justice.'

Then they heard the distant roar of the engines of the huge plane due to leave for Rio de Janeiro at 1500 hours.

Angel checked his watch again. It was exactly three o'clock.

The armed PC said, 'Do you want to see it take off?'

He directed them to an outdoor balcony. They pressed forward to try to get a good position. They were packed in tightly with fifty or sixty people: other sightseers. They lifted themselves out of their shoes when a plane took off. Most everyone was exhilarated watching the planes taxiing here and there, taking off and landing.

The plane for Rio de Janeiro roared away.

The PC said, 'It can get really interesting. Last week a plane was turned back because it was losing fuel . . . splashed some of the crowd watching it.'

Angel was absolutely devastated as he saw the plane disappear into the clouds. He had broken all sorts of rules. Harker would have gone mad if he knew the short cuts he had taken. It was a complete disaster as far as he was concerned. He was downcast, disappointed, thoughtful and strangely quiet.

Flora turned to Angel and said, 'You did your best. There's nothing more we can do here.'

Then the PC said, 'The plane will come back in a minute and fly over us . . . if you wait you can see it again.'

Then he made his way back to the wall behind and, ever vigilant, observed the crowds, his rifle always at the ready.

Angel's face suddenly brightened. He turned to Flora and whispered, 'Follow what I do and say.'

She frowned.

He turned away.

They waited.

The plane returned and passed over them high in the sky.

Everybody looked up — some marvelled at the sight.

Angel suddenly yelled, 'Oow!'

He reached for his handkerchief and began rubbing his eyes.

'Oow, petrol or diesel,' he said. 'It stings.'

Flora turned away and searched her pocket for a presentable tissue. She found one and began rubbing her eyes also.

'From that plane,' Angel said, pointing upwards and still wiping. 'Petrol or something like that . . . Can't see . . .'

A young man squashed next to him began to wipe his eyes also. 'I think I caught a splash,' he said. 'Is it kerosene?'

The woman with him said, 'I didn't notice anything.'

A man the other side of her said, 'There *was* something, look at my coat. That shoulder is wet,' he said and took out his handkerchief.

Another man behind Angel, brandishing his handkerchief said, 'It's a special aeroplane fuel. Yes. My eyes are smarting.' He rubbed his eyes vigorously.

Interest was spreading fast . . .

The armed PC noticed saw the activity of the group and pushed his way through the crowd to Angel and said, 'What's happening?'

Angel continued rubbing his eyes and pulled a face of pain.

The young man next to Angel tugged the PC's coat sleeve and said, 'I can tell you. That plane that just went over must have been leaking fuel. It splashed a lot of people. It's not—'

The armed PC's eyes flashed. '*Leaking fuel!*'

He looked around and saw many of the crowd wiping their eyes or brandishing their handkerchiefs or tissues.

He winked at Angel, then to the young man he said, 'I must report this. Will you come with me, sir?'

'Of course,' the young man said, pleased to be suddenly in the midst of a drama.

The PC pushed his way through the crowd. 'Excuse me,' he said. 'Excuse me . . . quickly, please . . . quickly, please . . . thank you . . . this is an emergency . . . thank you . . . thank you.'

The young man dutifully followed. They rushed away. The PC was talking most urgently on his radio telephone as they went.

Flora turned to Angel and quietly said, 'What are you up to? As if I didn't know.'

Angel tapped in a number on his phone to the airport security office and while he waited for a reply said, in a quiet voice, 'Well, cross your fingers . . . let's see if it works.'

There was a response from the phone.

'Is that the airport security office? Can I speak urgently to the duty officer? I am Detective Inspector Angel from Bromersley Police. Will you please help me on a very serious matter that is urgent?'

* * *

Twelve minutes later, the three o'clock plane to Rio de Janeiro returned to the airport and after landing on the tarmac runway number one, the senior flight attendant made an announcement to passengers of the plane through the PA.

'Ladies and gentlemen, my name is Elaine and I want to bring you up to date. You may unfasten your seat belts and relax for ten or fifteen minutes. When everything is ready, I will ask you to pick up your hand luggage and prepare to disembark. We may be travelling in this plane or another at a later time. This has to be arranged and will take a little time. Please retire to the restaurant where you will be served afternoon tea with the compliments of British Airways.'

The passengers remained seated but grumbled among themselves for a while.

Margaret Mountjoy put down her very thick paperback — *The Biography of Errol Flynn* — turned to Maurice and said, 'That's nice. I could just do with a cup of tea.'

Her husband grunted, 'Mmm. I don't know. I wish we were over the Atlantic.'

Margaret looked at him and said, 'The trouble with you, Maurice, is that you're never satisfied.'

She returned to Errol Flynn.

Maurice Mountjoy glanced out through a small window at the runway and saw at the barrier two security policemen each armed with a Heckler carbine. Their eyes were on the plane. He thought there was no doubt that they also had a Glock handgun, a Taser and a CS gas canister each. Also, he thought there were probably at least two more somewhere in the vicinity.

He looked around and saw a small goods car towing three low, empty trailers being driven by a uniformed luggage handler towards a pile of luggage standing on the tarmac by the next plane. He looked again at the driver of the small goods car. There was something familiar about the driver. He looked again at his face. It looked like Michael Angel. It looked *just* like Michael Angel.

It *was* Michael Angel!

Maurice Mountjoy's jaw dropped. His eyes swivelled as he urgently considered what to do.

He turned to his brother Eric sitting next to him and whispered, 'Have you . . . erm, recovered the gun?'

'No,' he replied.

Maurice's face muscles tightened angrily. 'Well get to the—' he nodded towards the toilets — 'and *retrieve it double quick*,' he snapped. 'And give those mucky hands a good wash. It's time you got that paint off round your nails. And hurry up.'

Eric stood up sulkily, pushed past him, down the aisle to the toilet. There were three. He tried the doors. They were all locked . . . all engaged.

A big man in a kilt came up to him and said, 'There's a queue here, laddie, and I'm next. And that woman over there is after me.'

Eric looked down the length of the plane and discovered that between the many heads and shoulders, they could see each other. In fact, Maurice was watching him. Eric looked back at Maurice who sniffed, turned away, shoved his hands in his pockets and leaned back against a mock-wooden panel.

The panel gave way — turned out not to be a panel at all, but the door to the pilot's cabin. The door opened wide and Eric went in with it. He staggered backwards and finished up inside still holding onto the door. The two pilots who were seated, checking off notes against instrument readings, stared up at him in alarm. He looked back at them like a surprised rabbit.

'I'm sorry, sir, but you must leave at once,' the younger one of the pilots said, removing his headphones. He stood up. 'This is out of bounds to passengers.'

Eric blinked. His face went red. He looked at the floor then the door and went out of the cabin.

The pilot then quickly closed the door and locked it.

Maurice had seen all this. Also, through the window, he had observed the taxiing of the mobile staircase to the plane's passenger door. The corners of his mouth turned down. Matters were moving too fast . . . and getting out of hand. He must get the plane in the air.

A few minutes later, Eric was able to access one of the toilet cubicles. He rushed inside and locked the door. He unfastened his trousers, lowered them and was able to peel off a large plaster from his groin and take out a small but deadly Beretta handgun. He pushed it into his jacket pocket, adjusted his clothes and returned to his seat next to Maurice and Margaret.

Maurice looked at Margaret. She was thoroughly engrossed in her paperback.

He turned to Eric seated next to him. 'Have you got it?' Maurice said.

'It's in my pocket,' Eric said.

'Give it to me. Careful. Pass it to me under that newspaper.'

Maurice quickly grabbed the gun, put it in his own pocket, stood up.

Eric said, 'Where are you going?'

Maurice said, 'Stay here with Margaret. She will tell you what to do.'

'Will you be long?'

'If you want anything, *ask* her.'

Eric lowered his eyebrows. He looked at Margaret . . . she was completely oblivious to everything except the book. He looked up at Maurice who was roughly pushing in front of her to pass.

She looked up from her book, her lips tightened briefly, she moved her knees to one side to let him through then put her head back into the book.

Maurice strode boldly down the plane to the pilot's cabin. He tried the door but it was locked. He knocked on it.

A voice said, 'Who is it?'

He said, 'Police. Very urgent.'

'Just a minute.'

Mountjoy heard the door being unlocked. It opened several centimetres and the face of the younger pilot appeared.

Mountjoy put the gun to the pilot's nose and said, 'Open this door.'

The man stared down the barrel of the gun, slowly pulled open the door and backed away.

Mountjoy went into the cabin, pushed the pilot in the chest, pointed the gun at him and said, 'Sit down.'

He closed the door without looking at it, felt for the key and locked it.

Then he said, 'Now both of you listen. I want you to get this plane in the air in double quick time.'

The two pilots looked at each other and the older one said, 'It's *impossible*.'

'Oh no. Oh no. I'll tell you what's impossible,' Mountjoy said, looking at the older one. 'If you don't get this plane moving very, *very* soon, it will be impossible for you to stop me from shooting your colleague in the head. *That's* entirely possible. As you may need some assurance that I mean what I say, I will spend very valuable time telling that I have murdered four people very recently, and I am therefore wanted by the police. One more murder charge would make no difference. So *get on with it!*'

The older one said, 'We can't. For a start, we have to get permission from security and from the tower.'

'I'm giving you permission from both. *Get on with it!*'

'We've to check the fuel. We've been told there's a leak.'

'The fuel's all right,' he said. '*You're trying my patience!*'

'Well . . . it'd be downright dangerous. The runway may not be clear. There are scores of take-offs and landings twenty-four/seven.'

'It will be all right. Take it from me. *Get on with it!*'

'What's our bearings? We can't aim for Rio. We may not have sufficient fuel. I've seventy-two passengers out there that I have to consider.'

'I haven't. Just get it airborne, Biggles, before I run out of patience.'

'Yes, but do I point north, south, east or west?'

Mountjoy pointed the gun with a jerk at the younger pilot's head and said, 'Any direction you like. If you don't start those engines in the next two minutes, your friend here will never *ever* have the need to worry again.'

On hearing the plane's engines, the team outside manoeuvring the staircase quickly pulled it away from the side of the plane to safeguard the wing and tail.

The plane began to roll forward.

Inside the plane, the older pilot looked away from the runway to Mountjoy and said, 'We cannot enter a runway without the tower's permission.'

Mountjoy's top lip tightened against his teeth. 'I give you *my* permission,' he growled. 'Get up there!'

'But *it's dangerous* . . . other planes might be around . . . coming or going . . . using the *same* airspace.'

Mountjoy's face went scarlet. He pointed the gun ten centimetres away from the young pilot's head and pulled the trigger.

Hot lead shot through the air and landed in the imitation wood partition.

In the confined space of the cabin the sound of the shot was deafening.

Both pilots gasped.

Passengers at the other side of the partition heard it. Some thought it was from the engines.

Mountjoy said to the older pilot, 'How many more times do I have to tell you to get this bloody plane airborne? If you don't, I promise you that your young friend here will be shaking hands with Saint Peter at the pearly gates very much earlier than his mother ever expected. Now *move!*'

Meanwhile, the staircase outside the plane with Angel on the top step had been pushed towards the passenger door of the plane.

The plane began to move.

The senior flight attendant, Elaine, saw him through the window, promptly opened the plane door and Angel tried to reach across the open divide to board the plane, just as he heard the roar of the engine causing the plane to shake.

He looked down. The ground was moving beneath him. It was a ten-metre drop onto a very hard surface.

He quickly grabbed the handrail and swung himself towards the plane.

Elaine snatched hold of his coat and pulled him inside. Then she closed the door and said, 'That was a very risky thing to do. Are you all right?'

Angel leaned forward, panting. He took several breaths then said, 'Yeah.'

He looked round then, after a few seconds, he looked through the window outside. The ground staff were quickly pulling the staircase away.

'Thank you, miss,' Angel said.

'My name's Elaine,' she said.

'Elaine. That's a nice name,' Angel said then he added, 'Tell me. Why is the plane on the move?'

'We have no idea. I've rung the office and they don't know either. And they can't make contact with the pilots.'

On seeing the plane's wheels move, the team outside on the tarmac quickly pulled the staircase away from the side of the plane.

Elaine said, 'Who are you, sir?'

'My name is Michael Angel. I am a police inspector. You have a man — a passenger with his wife and another. I have to arrest them.'

Angel noticed some of the passengers and the flight crew began to gather round them and were listening to what was being said.

Elaine turned and found two big ladies standing very close almost touching her.

'Excuse me,' she said. 'Excuse me. Thank you.'

The big ladies grudgingly moved. She was then able to reach the tuck-away desktop. On it was a clipboard. She picked it up.

'What's his name?' she said.

'Mountjoy.'

She began to look down the clipboard.

'What did he do?'

'Murdered four people.'

Elaine's mouth dropped. Comments from the crowd came thick and fast.

Elaine suddenly looked up from her list, pointed at the pilot's cabin and said, 'He's in there. And you can't get in. The door's locked and he won't open it for anything.'

Angel sighed. 'Tell me what you know about him. Every little thing.'

The plane was still rolling forward.

The engines roared.

Inside the plane, Elaine had instructed the passengers to put on their seat belts.

The plane taxied onto the runway and began to gather speed. They were halfway down the runway when another plane passed very noisily, closely and quickly overhead, momentarily unnerving Mountjoy, the pilots and the bewildered passengers.

There was a smaller plane coming up in front of them. Mountjoy's plane was ten or fifteen metres from the tarmac when the older pilot saw it. It was at about the same height.

The two pilots exchanged worried glances.

Would the smaller plane be increasing its height just as they were overtaking it? They were only a few seconds away. They quickly struggled to make the plane a few metres higher but it flew very closely over the other plane. The pilots held their breaths. They heard several scratching sounds coming from underneath as it passed. They waited for trouble. They looked at their extensive instrument panel. Then blew out a length of air. They seemed to have got away with it.

As they climbed higher, the pilots soon found some empty sky, and luckily it was a clear day.

Mountjoy looked at the older pilot and said, 'That's high enough. Now level off and aim north.'

The pilot shuffled uneasily, looked at the compass and changed the direction of the plane to north as marked.

Mountjoy looked over his shoulder at the compass, then said, 'I've employed hundreds of smart arses like you. I've taken men and women from the huge pool of out-of-work actors and singers in this country. And I have paid skilled writers to put words in their mouths, top musicians to write magical music and accomplished professionals to teach them how to sing. If they mimed a short-lived popular song, they could be made for life. Some, I paid out a fortune for a mouthful of shiny false teeth, a glamorous wig, a quick slimming treatment, a course of hair extensions and anything else that cropped up to make a Maid Marion out of a potato picker. Then I starred them in a film. Weeks afterwards, they became stars and celebrities. In great demand . . . wanted and feted wherever they went. And they honestly believe it's because they are so wonderful.

'They forget that *I* put them there.'

SEVENTEEN

Angel was in the plane's flight staff room, considering what to do.

He was mulling over everything that Elaine had been able to tell him about the situation. He was aghast to learn that Mountjoy had a gun. Eventually, he turned to Elaine and said, 'Have you got — or do you know where I can get — a short piece of metal tubing?'

'What do you want that for?' she said.

'An idea I've got. Haven't you any toolboxes?'

'They're in the pilot's cabin.'

Obviously they were inaccessible.

'Or remains from repairs or servicing . . . you know? Have the plane's gas or liquid pipes recently been changed or repaired and the bits not thrown away?'

'No. Can't think of anything. They always clear up after themselves.'

'Mmm, 'Angel said. He looked down and closed his eyes in concentration for a few seconds. Then suddenly he looked up . . . his eyes shining with excitement.

'Have you got a lipstick?' he said.

Her eyebrows shot up. She swiftly turned to look directly into his face.

'Have you got a lipstick?' he repeated.

She reached into her handbag and came out with a gilt and black lipstick case. She held it up.

He stared at it. 'Ah,' he said and his eyes sparkled with the delight of a rat in a dustbin.

She passed it to him.

He suddenly felt rejuvenated by adrenaline.

He unscrewed it and took out the red stick on its base and passed that part of it back to Elaine, retaining the gilt and black top.

Angel looked at the top ... turned it every which way ... pressed it on the back of his hand ... then banged it hard down onto his knee. Then he slipped the top into his pocket.

Elaine had watched every move and was more mystified than ever.

'Will it do?' she said.

Angel was slow to reply. 'I am not sure,' he said. Then he said, 'The Mountjoys were a party of three. Where are the other two?'

'Halfway down the plane on your left. They're in forty-three, forty-four and forty-five. The woman has blonde hair and is wearing an expensive white coat over a blue dress. The man is small, has a big mop of uncontrolled dark hair and is wearing a dark raincoat.'

Angel nodded. He walked casually down the plane, closely observed by passengers who were not watching television.

He glanced at the Mountjoys and saw Margaret with her nose in a book, and Eric watching a TV film.

He returned to Elaine in the staff room.

'How did you find them?' she said.

'They are bound to be loyal to Maurice,' he said thoughtfully.

'What do you want to do?'

'Have you a little room we can put them in?'

Elaine said, 'There's the staff room, the galley and the pantry.'

'What's that room like a cupboard next to the staff room?'

'That's the pantry. It *is* a store cupboard. We keep everything in there.'

Angel frowned. 'Everything? What sort of everything?'

'Everything.'

Angel said, 'Can I take a look?'

Elaine said, 'Follow me.'

Angel followed her out of the staff room and round the corner to the pantry between the staff room door and the pilot's cabin.

He looked in surprise at its size and also how much it stocked. The pantry was the size of a massive Victorian kitchen cupboard with very short, stubby feet a centimetre from the floor to two metres, with two very wide hardboard doors.

He considered too how much kit was needed simply to fly a passenger aircraft. He could see fire hoses, emergency heavy rescue tools, inflatable life rafts, refrigerators, stationary, hostess trolleys, children's chairs, serviettes, crates of beer, wines, and whisky, buckets and mops and dry goods such as currants, raisins, cooking oil . . .

He scratched his head.

Elaine said, 'Well, what are you thinking?'

He said, 'If some of that stuff was better stacked and some brought out, it would be possible to make space to conceal Margaret and Eric Mountjoy on chairs in there for a short period of time.'

Elaine looked surprised and didn't know what to say.

Angel stroked his chin, looked at her and said, 'Could you organise that if I find you four strong men to do the work?'

She shook her head, then nodded and said, 'I suppose so.'

Angel changed his mind. 'No. It's not fair. You've done enough,' he said. 'I'll do it, but thank you, love.'

She smiled and eagerly said, 'I'll help.'

'Well, I'll need some lengths of rope and two scarves.'

'I can do that,' she said.

'Good,' he said. 'Now, have you any paraffin?'

Elaine's jaw dropped. 'You ask me for the strangest things,' she said.

He repeated more urgently, 'Have you any paraffin?'

'No. Of course I haven't. It would be highly dangerous to have such stuff here on a plane.'

'Well . . . have you access to any petrol, kerosene, lighter fuel or similar inflammable liquid?'

'Certainly not. No.'

'Right,' he said.

Then he went to the front of the plane and said, 'Can I have your attention, please?'

Everybody looked up. If they had been talking they stopped.

'You have been very patient. I won't keep you long, I am a police officer and I know that you want this plane to return to London for refuelling and then fly on to Rio.'

'Yes. Yes,' some of the passengers said.

'Well, I want to arrest a man who is a multiple murderer and in the pilots' cabin with a gun pointed at the pilots, intending to make his getaway to I know not where, but not London and not Rio.'

204

There were a few gasps from the passengers.

'I have a plan that will hopefully get him out of there, but I will need a lot of help. Firstly, I need volunteers . . . four strong men to quickly move some stock around to make more space.'

Many of the men, bored with the journey and needing to exercise their limbs, put up their hands.

He chose the nearest four and said, 'Thank you all very much. Will you come with me?'

He opened the big pantry doors and gazed at all it stocked.

In five long minutes Angel and the men had inflatable dinghies and other stuff packed high on the refrigerators and crates of wines and spirits stacked on each other with stuff on top of them.

'Thanks very much,' he said to the men. 'It's a good job. I need two of you to come with me on another little job.'

Angel and the two helpers went to the middle of the plane to Margaret and Eric. Margaret was still reading the book and Eric was still engrossed in the TV. In view of their name and relationship with Maurice Mountjoy, they had been keeping a very low profile.

'Now you two come with me,' Angel said.

Eric, expressionless, stood up ready.

'Where to?' Margaret said, still holding the book and staying firmly in her seat.

Angel said, 'If you don't come voluntarily, I have two strong men to carry you.'

'Oh!' she said, shocked at the thought and stood up. 'What about Eric, my brother-in-law?'

'Yes. I am going to hide you both for a little while . . . perhaps half an hour at the most. You'll be together.'

Margaret seemed to have accepted the situation. He noticed she held onto the book.

'I should leave your book here,' he said. 'You won't be able to read it. You can finish it afterwards.'

She reluctantly left the book on her seat.

Angel directed the two Mountjoys along to the front of the plane.

Elaine had found two chairs which she put inside the pantry next to each other. Angel rearranged them. He put one each side of the pantry and facing the doors when they were closed so that they couldn't assist each other to escape.

Angel roped Eric to the chair, tied it round his waist, round his wrists and around his ankles. Then he put the scarf across his mouth and pulled it tight. He checked that his nostrils were not covered.

Elaine had watched Angel tying up Eric and copied all the moves tying up Margaret and putting a scarf across her mouth. Angel checked her fastenings and that Margaret's nostrils were not covered with the scarf. He was anxious that neither of the Mountjoys would get free and warn Maurice of the trap set for him.

Angel gave them one last check over. Then he closed the big pantry doors and returned to the front of the front of the plane.

They all went silent when they saw Angel standing there waiting to speak.

'Friends,' he began. 'I was saying that I want to arrest this multiple murderer who is in the pilots' cabin with a gun pointed at the pilots, intending to make his getaway to somewhere north but not London and not Rio. However, between us we can get him out of there.

'Simply knocking on the door with all sorts of reasons, excuses and offers won't succeed. To answer the door would require him to take his eyes off the pilots for a couple of seconds, which for him might be too long. We have to rouse his curiosity to such a pitch that he will be compelled to open the door voluntarily.'

The big Scotsman in the kilt stood up and said, 'Aye . . . well . . . how can we do that?'

'Well, a fire would be good but even a small one would be dangerous. I can't take that risk. But it would be great to put him in *fear* of one . . . I'm going to ask for volunteers. Don't scream now, please, but by a show of hands, are there any ladies who can scream at a high pitch and loudly?'

Two hands shot up, quickly followed by two more, then several others after that.

'Thank you. I should think three or four will be enough. Will you first four come forward and stay together there?'

Five ladies of various ages arrived but Angel didn't send the last one back. He picked a position near the staff room door and said, 'We can't rehearse because it will give the show away. But when I say, "Cue screamers," I want each of you to immediately give one shrill, piercing scream. One only. That's all.'

Then he turned back to the body of passengers and said, 'Now it's the turn of you men. I need five singers who usually sing bass,' he said.

There was no response.

Angel said, 'Come on, gentlemen. I'm not going to ask you to sing solo or anything like that. Just to shout out loudly.'

The big Scotsman came forward and said, 'I can do that. I'm bass.'

Angel smiled at him and said, 'Great.'

The Scotsman turned to face the passengers and said, 'Come along, you pasty-faced, chicken-hearted Sassenachs. Put your vanity in your pocket and let's help this young copper . . . and ourselves.'

Several hands went up straightaway. Then several more.

Angel said, 'You first five come forward. Are you all in good voice?'

They mostly nodded or muttered, 'Yes.'

Angel said, 'There are two jobs I want you to do. The first one is the simulation of an explosion. We have to create the loudest bang and vibration we can muster. It has to be one thrust only. And directly on that thin dividing wall that creates the pilot's cabin. We must use both hands — not fists — and our bodies at one thrust. Not yet, but in a few moments. All right?

'Will you please turn and face me? Now, I'm going to give each of you words to shout as loud as you can and just the once. All right?'

Angel went down the line. 'This is what you say, "What's happened?", "What's the matter?" "It's a fire." "What?" "It's a fire." "Where?" "Oh help. Help. It's a fire." "Oh my God! Where's the fire?" You shout those phrases when I cue you. I'll do that by putting my hand on your shoulder. Stop shouting when I ask you.'

Angel turned back to the passengers and said, 'The last thing. Has anybody got any cellophane? The sort of stuff that's round a box of chocolates or maybe teabags or some wrapped-up box of most any sort?'

Several sheets were soon forwarded to the front and handed to Angel.

'Thank you,' he said. 'Thank you. One sheet would be enough.'

He gave them to Elaine and spoke quietly to her for a few seconds, then he turned back to the passengers and said, 'Now, everybody has a part to play, please. When I cue you, I want you to stay in your seats but shuffle your feet on the floor or bang them to simulate you are moving around and hit irregularly anything to make a noise that might suggest to the man with the gun in the pilot's cabin that there is panic in the plane. All right?'

Nobody replied.

Angel looked at them and smiled. 'Everybody! Will you — can you — do that, please?'

A few voices said, 'Yes.'

'I would like *everybody* to join in. Will you make noise with your feet on the floor when I ask you to?'

A lot more voices said, 'Yes.'

'Thank you.'

Elaine switched on the microphone and hung it on the partition and nodded and smiled at Angel indicating that she was ready.

'Now, are we all ready to play our part? Is everybody ready to go?'

He looked round.

It was remarkably quiet. But most of the passengers were paying attention.

He asked the men to put their hands on the panels around the walls of the pilot's cabin, like hugging a tree. He did likewise. Then he said, 'I'll quietly say, *one, two, three* and then *now*!'

He looked back and said, 'Are you screamers ready?'

'Yes. Yes,' several of them replied.

'Here we go then, everybody,' he said. 'Men. Remember only one quick loud bang. Are we ready? I'll count us in. One, two. three, *NOW*!'

The men made quite a racket which also shook the partition.

Angel enjoyed the small part he played.

He turned to the women at the front and said, 'Screamers, your cue *now*!'

The ladies made a terrific job of screaming. They were so loud and shrill. Angel thought they had the taken the colour out of his tie.

Then he immediately cued the men to begin shouting about the fire.

Then he nodded to Elaine to crumple the cellophane in her hands in front of the microphone to simulate a crackling fire.

And the passengers began banging and shuffling their feet and making plenty of noise.

Angel quickly backed off into the staff room, hopefully awaiting some reaction from the gunman.

It wasn't long before the pilot's cabin door was opened and the younger of the pilots could be seen. He had his hands in the air and was very closely followed by Mountjoy holding the gun in his back.

Angel held his breath. He could hear the rapid throbbing of his pulse in his ears.

The passengers instantly became silent, many faces showing astonishment with open mouths, raised eyebrows and staring eyes.

Maurice Mountjoy's face became visible as he peered from behind the pilot. They advanced through the doorway a centimetre at a time.

Angel held his breath as he peered at him and his hostage through the slit between the door and the door jamb of the partly open staff room door. He thought Mountjoy looked very nervous.

Angel needed to get behind Mountjoy to overwhelm him. It required Mountjoy to move forward a couple of metres at least.

Mountjoy pushed the pilot forward a little and, peering from behind him, said, 'Listen up, you people . . . you lovely people. This is a gun I am holding and this man, who is the co-pilot, is my prisoner. If anybody tries to attack me, the safety catch is off, I will shoot this man and use the rest of the bullets to defend myself. *Understand that.* I have killed before so I am not squeamish. I would kill again. Now, a few moments ago there was an explosion and, it seemed, a fire. I was very concerned for you all and wondered what had happened.'

Mountjoy glanced at the passengers immediately in front of them and pushed the pilot forward towards them.

Angel noted that it still wasn't far enough for him to get directly behind Mountjoy. However, he saw the gun for the first time. It was only small. It didn't make it any the less deadly. He thought it might be a Beretta Tomcat. He could be wrong. He couldn't see much of it. But from memory its magazine held seven rounds. He bit his lip.

Mountjoy didn't seem to favour that side of the plane because Angel saw him tugging the pilot's shirt, directing him to turn through ninety degrees. It looked as if he was intending to head past the pantry doors over to the side where the staff room was and from where Angel was observing him. Maybe providence was sending him a golden opportunity!

Angel's heart beat faster.

Then, in the quiet, he heard a soft but distinctive banging noise like a gloved hand or foot on a wooden door. It was repeated. It sounded like it was coming from the pantry door.

Then, suddenly, he saw a red-faced Mountjoy turn, push the pilot to one side and fire the gun at the door.

Bang!

Angel gasped.

Mountjoy stared at the door, pointed the gun at it and shouted, 'Come out, you bloody coward! Come out where I can see you. Do you want some more? Come out! Face up to me like a man.'

He fired three more shots.

Bang! Bang! Bang!

Angel's heart sank. He recalled that those pantry doors were only thin hardboard.

The passengers remained speechless and motionless in their seats, watching every move the man with the gun made.

Then Mountjoy, gun in hand, went up to the pantry doors and pulled open the one he had fired into. He didn't open it far. He just peered into it for a few moments.

Angel saw a trickle of blood drip over the pantry step. He felt his stomach turn over. Eric must surely be hit.

Mountjoy closed the pantry door and turned away. The sight didn't seem to register with him. He seemed simply not to care. Maybe he didn't realise that Eric had been trying to warn him of the trap to disarm him.

Mountjoy looked round for the young pilot.

He was nowhere to be seen.

Mountjoy stood there, facing the passengers and pointing the gun downwards.

He put up his other hand. He wanted to speak.

If he stayed in that position it was a chance for Angel to overcome him.

Angel's speed of breathing increased. It was the excitement . . . the anticipation. He could take Mountjoy.

'Friends,' he began. 'You can see what I've had to do. I had to fire into a cupboard not knowing that they have a man in there actually tied up with a rope.'

Angel took out the lipstick cover from his pocket, tiptoed silently out of the staff room up to the back of Mountjoy, pushed it hard into his coccyx, and said, 'One false move and you will spend the rest of your life in a wheelchair.'

Mountjoy's eyes centred and shone. 'Who's that? That's not Angel,' he said. 'Can't be. Left you at the airport. In London.'

'Drop the gun.'

He didn't.

Angel pressed the lipstick cover harder into his coccyx, hoping he would believe it was a gun.

'Drop the gun.'

Mountjoy dropped the gun.

Angel kicked it a couple of feet away. Then he retrieved it. He wasn't taking any chances of being kicked in the face while he was bent down picking it up.

He dropped the lipstick cover into his pocket, pointed the gun at Mountjoy and said, 'Turn round and put your hands behind your back.'

Next, Angel took a pair of handcuffs out of his pocket and deftly fitted them round Mountjoy's wrists.

Angel then put the gun into his pocket.

It was at that point that the passengers all cheered and waved their books, papers, shirts or pants in the air. Many of them smiled widely and one or two yelled, 'Good old Angel!'

The big Scotsman stood up, turned and said, 'A Sassenach we can be proud of!'

Elaine came up to Angel, glanced at the sullen, pasty-faced Mountjoy, and gave Angel a kiss on the cheek.

Angel was pleased and surprised but he remained nervous and cool when he said, 'Will you get Mrs Mountjoy out of the pantry and make her comfortable?'

Elaine nodded and then said, 'Of course. Is she under arrest?'

Angel said, 'Certainly not. There are no charges against her. We shall want her back as a witness, but she is as free as a bird.'

She went off to the pantry.

Amidst all the ruckus, Angel called out to the Scotsman, 'Will you hold the gun on this Mountjoy for a minute or two? If he moves at all or gives you any trouble just pull the trigger.'

'I'd be delighted, laddie. Give it to me. I'm more used to a rifle . . . shooting grouse, you ken, but the principle is the same.'

He gave the Scotsman the gun and said, 'I want to see if there is any life in that poor man in the pantry.'

'Take as long as you need,' the Scotsman said.

Angel crossed quickly to the pantry.

Elaine had already cut the rope fastenings around Margaret Mountjoy and assisted her out of the chair and out of the pantry.

'Thank you, my dear,' she said. 'I want to return to my comfortable seat number forty-four, if that's all right?' she said.

'It's perfectly all right,' Elaine said. 'Inspector Angel said there are no charges at all against you . . . you are as free as a bird.'

Then Elaine led her up the aisle.

Margaret's face altered. Her eyes hardened. The corners of her mouth turned downward. 'But he murdered dear Eric, then, did he?' she said.

Elaine couldn't think of any alternative word to say other than, 'Yes.'

'He murdered his own brother and he doesn't give a fig.'

'I'm sure he didn't mean to . . . I think he thought that someone was hiding there . . . someone who had planned to come out unexpectedly and overcome him.'

Her face remained sad until they arrived at her seat and she saw her book just as she had left it. She picked it up and looked at the page. Her face lit up and she quickly sat down against the two empty seats and began to read.

Elaine said, 'Are you all right now?'

'Yes, thank you,' she said. 'I'll be all right.'

Elaine returned down the aisle to the front of the plane.

Meanwhile, Angel had opened the other door pantry door to reveal a ghastly sight. Blood all over . . . even on the door. Eric Mountjoy still tied to the chair. His skin all shiny . . . mouth wide open . . . false teeth sticking out . . . more blood on his shirt . . . blood on his coat . . . trousers . . . blood everywhere . . . on the floor.

Angel put his fingertips gently on Eric's neck, feeling for a pulse — a bit pointless, he thought, but he must be certain . . . Nothing.

He closed the pantry door. He was sad, but he knew keeping busy was the right medicine for him.

Elaine came up to him and said, 'Margaret Mountjoy is all right, now.'

'Thank you. You are a great help,' he said then he added, 'Where is the young pilot?'

'Where all good pilots go,' she said. 'He's back in the cockpit. He and the other pilot are making it hell for leather back to London. He said we should be there in an hour.'

Angel raised his eyebrows and said, 'Oh great.'

EIGHTEEN

Angel quickly settled all the necessary urgent business at Heathrow Airport and was offered free, two of the four unsold seats on Pandora Airways regular weekday 1700 hours service to Leeds Bradford airport for him to bring Maurice Mountjoy back to Bromersley.

The back seats were taken by Angel and Mountjoy handcuffed to each other.

The two men didn't talk to each other and they only said what was absolutely necessary.

After about twenty minutes on the road, Angel looked out of the window and stifled a yawn.

Mountjoy noticed this and after a little while said, 'Well, Angel, what happens to me next?'

Angel looked at him and shrugged. He didn't want to answer him. He wasn't disposed to chat socially with him but said, 'You'll spend tonight in a cell in Bromersley Station.'

'Then what?'

Tomorrow you will go to the Magistrates' Court and when they hear your offences will hold you over for a Crown Court hearing, probably in Leeds.'

'What will happen there?'

'The judge will set a date for your trial. There I expect you'll get life.'

Mountjoy's fists tightened. He clenched his teeth and his voice changed to an animalistic growl. 'That'll please you,' he said, 'the copper, like the Mountie, who always gets his man! Damn you!'

Angel turned away.

Mountjoy continued.

'I intended getting my own back on you ever since I met you. I tried to puncture your ego by sending you letters to upset your equilibrium . . . to put a large measure of fear in your veins. I didn't sign them, of course.'

Angel listened intently. He was particularly interested to find that Mountjoy was the author of those disturbing anonymous letters with the Harrogate postmark.

'You might as well know about it,' Mountjoy said. 'It doesn't matter now . . . I won't be making those trips up to Harrogate . . . won't be sending any more.'

* * *

A local patrol car was waiting at Bromersley Police Station to take the tired Angel home.

Angel and Mary exchanged relieved smiles and she quickly set him at ease after all the excitement of the day's events. He was appreciative of the way she kept their home life relatively calm and peaceful. It was usually like that except when her divorced sister and her two children came to visit.

He finished a delightful dinner and walked into the sitting room of their little bungalow. He saw a newspaper on the sofa and picked it up. He checked the dateline. Wednesday,1 December. That was right. He looked at the headlines. *THREAT OF WORLD WAR. BILLIONS FOR NATIONAL HEALTH SERVICE. TV STAR ON RAPE CHARGE.*

He opened the paper and looked inside. A headline on page two grabbed his attention. It read, *DISASTER FILM RESCUED — 100 JOBS SAVED.* It went on to say that because of the notoriety surrounding the murders of some of the principals and crew of the new epic film, there had been so much public interest that the Giant Film Corporation had taken over production of the film with the appointment of replacement new leading actors and crew.

Angel grinned from ear to ear. Then read it again.

He slowly lowered the paper onto the sofa and went back into the kitchen.

He went over to the fridge and took out a beer. He began whistling happily. Some phrases sounded like *Singin' in the Rain.*

Mary was putting some clean pots back in the cupboard. He went over to her.

'What do you want, love?' she said.

'Just getting a glass,' he said with a smile.

She smiled back and said, 'What are you so happy about?'

'Oh, this and that.'

THE END

218

THE JOFFE BOOKS STORY

We began in 2014 when Jasper agreed to publish his mum's much-rejected romance novel and it became a bestseller.

Since then we've grown into the largest independent publisher in the UK. We're extremely proud to publish some of the very best writers in the world, including Joy Ellis, Faith Martin, Caro Ramsay, Helen Forrester, Simon Brett and Robert Goddard. Everyone at Joffe Books loves reading and we never forget that it all begins with the magic of an author telling a story.

We are proud to publish talented first-time authors, as well as established writers whose books we love introducing to a new generation of readers.

We won Trade Publisher of the Year at the Independent Publishing Awards in 2023 and Best Publisher Award in 2024 at the People's Book Prize. We have been shortlisted for Independent Publisher of the Year at the British Book Awards for the last five years, and were shortlisted for the Diversity and Inclusivity Award at the 2022 Independent Publishing Awards. In 2023 we were shortlisted for Publisher of the Year at the RNA Industry Awards, and in 2024 we were shortlisted at the CWA Daggers for the Best Crime and Mystery Publisher.

We built this company with your help, and we love to hear from you, so please email us about absolutely anything bookish at feedback@joffebooks.com.

If you want to receive free books every Friday and hear about all our new releases, join our mailing list here: www.joffebooks.com/freebooks.

And when you tell your friends about us, just remember: it's pronounced Joffe as in coffee or toffee!